She didn't want to fall for another man.

Especially one who had been clear from day one he had no intention of staying in Marique. They had nothing in common. Her family lived here. Her roots were in Marique. His were in America. She felt loyal to the king and crown. He actively disliked both.

If she ever felt in the position to risk her heart again, she'd want someone who shared her heritage and background. Someone easy to love and be loved by. Not the cauldron that was Jake White.

But sometimes the heart didn't listen to the head.

Barbara McMahon's latest novel is part of
a brand-new miniseries from Harlequin Romance®

Welcome to

*High Society
Brides*

The lives and loves of the royal, rich and famous!

We're inviting you to the most thrilling
and exclusive weddings of the year!

Meet women who have always wanted
the perfect wedding...but never dreamed that they
might be walking up the aisle with a millionaire,
an aristocrat, or even a prince!

But whether they were born into it, are faking it
or are just plain lucky—these women are about to be
whisked off around the world to the playground of
princes and playboys!

Are their dreams about to come true? If so, they
might just find that they are truly fit for a prince....

Look out for more HIGH SOCIETY BRIDES,
coming soon in Harlequin Romance®.

THE TYCOON PRINCE
Barbara McMahon

High Society
Brides

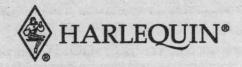

HARLEQUIN®

TORONTO • NEW YORK • LONDON
AMSTERDAM • PARIS • SYDNEY • HAMBURG
STOCKHOLM • ATHENS • TOKYO • MILAN • MADRID
PRAGUE • WARSAW • BUDAPEST • AUCKLAND

To Jessie Lee—
may you one day find your own wonderful prince!

ISBN 0-373-03753-8

THE TYCOON PRINCE

First North American Publication 2003.

This edition published by arrangement with Harlequin Books S.A.

® and TM are trademarks of the publisher. Trademarks indicated with
® are registered in the United States Patent and Trademark Office, the
Canadian Trade Marks Office and in other countries.

Visit us at www.eHarlequin.com

Printed in U.S.A.

CHAPTER ONE

THE shiny black limousine slid to a stop in the midst of battered pickup trucks, mud-splattered SUVs and potholes large enough to devour a man. Clarissa Dubonette stared in dismay at the construction site before her. Large sections of chain-link fence cordoned off the actual building site which was comprised of poured concrete and the tall wooden framework of what would one day become a shopping mall.

Not that she thought this section of California needed any more shopping malls. It seemed to her they'd passed one after another continually since they'd left the hotel earlier that morning.

She took a deep breath. She'd been the one entrusted with the mission. Time to carry forward. Studying the numerous construction workers, she searched in vain for a man who resembled Philippe. But while he had kept in shape playing polo, scuba diving and dancing the night away, his lean physique could never have compared with the muscular fitness of these construction workers.

Which one was Jake White?

She'd called the construction offices that morning and been told he was on site at this location. Imagining a handful of workers, she'd instructed the driver to bring her here. Instead, there had to be more than a hundred men at work. Some walked the high beams which would one day support a roof. Others poured concrete to enlarge the already huge footprint of the structure. Others were pulling wiring, or capping plumbing pipes. How in the world would she ever find him?

"Shall I ask someone about the gentleman?" the chauffeur asked after a long moment of silence while he, too, studied the scene before them.

"If you would. Jake White. The construction firm said he would be here. Maybe that man with the clipboard over there would know who he is." She couldn't imagine wandering around the site herself, calling his name.

"I'll find him." He climbed out of the limousine and walked over to the foreman. A moment of conversation and the man with the clipboard turned and hollered up to the top of the structure.

Clarissa followed his line of sight and saw a man slowly stand up and wave in acknowledgment. She held her breath as he nonchalantly walked along the narrow beam to a place where a ladder leaned against the board. He was easily twenty feet or more in the air, but walked as casually as if he were on terra firma.

He wore the required hard hat and apparently required hip-riding jeans that all the workers wore. But no shirt—it was tucked into the back of the waistband of those snug jeans. She swallowed hard. Quickly scanning the worksite, she noticed quite a few men had taken off their shirts in the hot California sun. Her eyes were drawn back to the one descending the ladder.

Maybe she was feeling prejudiced, but his shoulders seemed broader and browner than any others. The muscles moved beneath the skin as he made quick work of the ladder. His hair was mostly hidden by his hat, but a bit showed beneath the edge in back—black as sin. His hips were lean and his legs long and muscular.

When he reached the ground, he headed toward the chauffeur. Oh, Lord, Clarissa thought watching him, fascinated. It was like watching a panther on the prowl, lithe, sinuous and deadly dangerous. He had an earthiness about him that was mesmerizing. And totally inappropriate for the role he was to assume. He might have been raised in America, might have changed his name to an American version, but there was no mistaking who he was.

This was Jean-Antoine Simon Hercules LeBlanc, the future king of Marique.

She studied him as he walked across the dirt. He looked more like a sexy movie star who would have women swooning in a dozen countries. She swallowed hard and tried to cap her imagination and focus on her task. Subjects were definitely not supposed to fantasize about their future king! Did the current king have any idea what he was unleashing? She doubted it.

Mustering her poise, she opened the door and slipped out. It was not her place to wait for him to come to her.

She picked her way through the construction debris and rough ground. She heard a few whistles. Ignoring them, she kept her gaze fastened on the man now joining the chauffeur and foreman. He was even taller than she'd thought, more than six feet. Philippe had only been five ten, though he had carried himself so well he often looked taller.

She blanked out her memories. She would not think about Philippe. Not now when she was on a mission for her country. She'd been selected as emissary from the king. Her charge: bring home his grandson.

The king's view of the matter was that since she'd been engaged to Jake's cousin, and was part of the younger generation, she'd be the best suited to approach his grandson without the fanfare a more highly placed minister would evoke.

She knew the king was counting on her. She was aware of the honor it had been to be chosen. She wouldn't let him down!

The men stopped talking and turned to watch her approach. Jake White's gaze ran from her burnished auburn hair down to the expensive shoes on her feet. She thanked her years of training that allowed her to maintain her composure when faced with the dark sexy eyes that studied her so intently. Trying to ignore the feminine response that blossomed up so unexpectedly, she concentrated on her assignment.

"Carl said you wanted to see me," Jake said when she drew closer.

"Are you Jake White?"

"I am. Who are you?"

"Clarissa Dubonette. I'm representing His Majesty, Guilliam, King of Marique. Your grandfather."

His face darkened. "I have no grandfather." With that he turned to head back to work.

"Wait!" She blinked in surprise, astonished by his

response. This was not going at all the way she'd envisioned.

He turned back and raised an eyebrow.

"I believe I have the right man. Wasn't your mother Margaret Lansing? Your father Prince Joseph of Marique?"

He stared at her for a long minute then stepped forward, gripping her arm above the elbow and shepherding her away from the curiosity of the others. When they were out of hearing, he stopped.

"What do you want?"

"Are you the son—"

"Yeah, I'm Maggie and Joe's kid. So?"

The chip in his shoulder resembled one of California's fabled redwoods. She blinked. She thought he'd be thrilled to be contacted—to have his father's family recognize him at last.

She swallowed, aware of his grip on her arm, even through the jacket of her suit. Shimmering sensations tingled deep inside. She had trouble catching her breath. When she looked up into his dark eyes, she felt a stir of excitement from long-dormant emotions. His glittering gaze sparked an answering response in hers. For a moment the heat of the sun was nothing in comparison to the heat that washed through her.

She could almost imagine the construction site fading from view. That there were only the two of them alone on the planet—man and woman. Oh, she was in trouble.

Clarissa hadn't descended from generations of nobility to put up with this. She had her duty to perform! Raising her chin she pulled free and faced him, trying to keep her gaze firmly on those dark eyes and not on the bare chest inches in front of her nose.

Ignoring the firmly sculpted muscles that were so tantalizingly covered by an expanse of tanned skin, with a light dusting of dark hair, she locked her gaze with his. But that didn't stop all her other senses. She could smell his male scent above the sawdust and engine oil. It sparked an even greater awareness. Her skin still tingled from his grip. For a moment she wanted to reach out and touch—

Drawing a ragged breath, she focused on her task.

"His Majesty graciously requested I represent him in this task. He extends an invitation to visit Marique. I'm happy to escort you there." She fumbled pulling the letter from her shoulder bag, then offered it to Jake.

"I have no intentions of going to Marique. If that's all you came for, you wasted your time." He refused to reach for the envelope. Instead, his eyes skimmed over her again. Clarissa felt that kernel of heat grow, threatening to consume her. It had to be the hot Los Angeles sun. Or the blatant sexy look from the man facing her. She was used to more deference. And less open looks that zinged her blood to boiling level.

"But he needs you. The crown—"

"Needs me? That's a laugh. And even if it were true, I wouldn't go. Where was he when we needed him?"

"I don't know what you mean." This meeting was not going at all as Clarissa had expected. She had thought it a mere exercise in formality. A kindness the king had bestowed on her to offer her a chance to visit America and move on with her life. She really knew

very little about this man or his background. Only the
rare snippets Philippe had shared.

"I mean when my father died and my mother was left
alone and practically destitute to raise a kid with no help
from my father's family. I mean when she got sick and
I wrote to ask for help only to get my request slapped
back in my face. So you can take his invitation and—"

He stopped abruptly, obviously out of respect for her.
She could just imagine what he would have said to a
man.

"I'm not sure you understand. The crown prince and
his son have died. You are now heir to the throne. It's
time to come to Marique and assume your responsibilities," she tried to clarify.

Jake couldn't have been more stunned if she'd hit him
over the head with a two-by-four. His mother had told
stories about his father, the playboy prince who had married the Las Vegas showgirl. How dashing he'd been.
How wild. How romantic.

And how he'd tragically died so young in a racing
crash only months after his only son had been born.

She'd contacted the king, only to have him reject any
claims she had to his son's family, claiming he'd dis-
owned that son when he'd left home against his father's
express command. Once or twice she'd mentioned his
father's family—his older brother or that Jake had a
cousin a year or two older. When asked why they didn't
visit, she explained they lived so far away. It wasn't until
later that Jake learned the full truth.

Jake had grown up in the poorer section of Las Vegas,
while his mother worked double shifts to keep them in

food and clothing. He hadn't liked the stories she told—it made their situation seem all the more bleak knowing he had blood kin somewhere who had refused to recognize them.

Maggie had contracted breast cancer when Jake was a teenager. All the money in the world wouldn't have saved her. But a bit would have helped make her last months more comfortable. He'd written to his grandfather himself, only to have the letter returned.

Now that unfeeling snake wanted Jake to come and step into line for the monarchy?

"Not interested," he said, turning to walk away.

Why did that old man think Jake would ever want anything to do with him or his monarchy? Jake had by necessity grown up an American through and through, with no tangled feelings or loyalties for his father's birthplace. If the old man thought he was going to some tiny principality in the mountains between Spain and France, just because his grandfather suddenly needed him—or rather needed what he represented—the old man had another think coming.

For thirty-two years he'd repudiated Jake. Maybe now it was payback time. Didn't the old saying go, as you sow, so shall you reap?

"Please, let me explain." She did her best to keep up with him.

He stopped and glanced at his watch. Time was money in this business. It wasn't often he spent a day on site and he wanted to check out several more aspects, work with a couple of the new men to make sure they were up to his standards. He didn't have time to debate a nondebatable issue with some classy woman from Europe.

"I have things to do, even if you don't."

She flushed. "Of course. I'm sorry to interrupt your work. Would it be possible to discuss this later, when you are finished? At dinner, maybe?"

He almost smiled, glancing down at his faded jeans, his old, worn, comfortable work boots. "Sure you want it to be dinner?" he asked sardonically. Maybe he'd push the woman to see just how far she'd go to accomplish her mission.

"I'm happy to take you to dinner," she said quickly.

Did she think he needed someone else to buy his meals? Interesting. He had no intentions of agreeing to her virtual command to visit Marique. But dinner with a beautiful woman was not something to turn his nose up at, either. Especially with that fiery hair. The sun set it aflame, golds and reds and burnished copper fighting for domination.

"Dinner would work. Want me to pick you up?" He glanced around the dirt parking lot, motioned to the oldest, most battered pickup truck he saw. He didn't know to whom it belonged, but was curious as to her reaction. "Of course I don't have a limousine. But I do have wheels."

She glanced at the truck and barely contained a shudder. Jake almost laughed aloud. Who would have thought antagonizing one of his grandfather's minions would be so much fun? Maybe he'd string this out a bit and see where it led.

"I don't mind picking you up, if you like," she said politely. "I have hired a driver who knows the area."

"Or we can meet at a restaurant. You like ribs?"

She blinked again, her expression conveying her complete bafflement. He should caution her never to play poker.

"You know, barbequed ribs, lots of sauce dripping down? I know a great place in Van Nuys."

"If it's quiet so we can talk."

"Nah, it's raucous and boisterous. Lots of music, dancing, beer. But a lot of fun." He stepped closer. Would she back down?

She raised her chin again and Jake recognized defensive reactions when he saw them. Once again he was tempted to push the limits.

"I believe a quieter place would be more suitable." She didn't quite lift her nose in response, but he recognized snobbishness.

"Well, we could go to a hamburger joint or something. Bet we could find a quiet corner at one of those."

"Perhaps it would be better if we just dined at one of the restaurants in my hotel."

After a moment he agreed, more to end the discussion than because he had any desire to eat there. Teasing her was proving to be more fun than he would have thought, but he needed to get back to work.

She gave him the location of her hotel and they arranged to meet at seven. He watched as she walked carefully back to the limousine, picking her way over the boards and chunks of concrete that lay scattered around the uneven ground. He bet she wished she'd worn boots instead of those dainty high heels. Though the way she walked in them had every man in the area watching.

Once she slid into the limo and the driver closed the door, Jake realized he'd been staring at her the entire time himself. Granted, the way her hips moved did something to a man's libido, but she was strictly off-limits. And especially to him. He had a long-range plan for his life and the timing wasn't right for getting involved with a woman right now.

Besides, anyone representing his grandfather would be off-limits forever.

For a moment, the familiar anger threatened to surface. But Jake closed it off. He'd learned over the years it was useless. Nothing could change the way things were. He just wished he could do something to the old man to show him how he'd hurt his mother. To pay back the pain and anguish he'd caused over the years.

Jake shook his head, and headed back to check on one of the newest workers. This job was on schedule and under budget. He wanted to make sure it continued that way. Tomorrow he'd be back in the office, working on future projects, checking on other sites they had going, and dealing with the paperwork that was as relentless as the tide. It felt good, today, to be outside, to be swinging a hammer again, enjoying the camaraderie of other men who took pride in building structures to last. The time to plot and plan revenge had passed. He had other things to deal with now.

A few minutes before seven, Jake entered the plush lobby of Clarissa's hotel. He was early, wanting to be there when she arrived. He wondered if he called up if he would be invited to her room. He was tempted to try.

Stationing himself where he could watch the bank of elevators, he waited. He'd spent more of the afternoon than he'd wanted thinking about Clarissa's visit and invitation. Why hadn't his grandfather just called or written? Why send someone?

Probably because tradition dictated succession of the monarchy—not for any real desire on his part to contact Jake. If his uncle or cousin were still alive, Jake knew he never would have heard from his grandfather.

Had he thought to entice Jake into visiting by dangling the delectable Clarissa as additional bait? It didn't seem like something the woman would put up with—unless he'd misread the signs. Maybe dinner would give him more insight.

When Clarissa stepped from the elevator, he almost caught his breath. She had donned a dark blue evening dress, high around the neck, but cut away to display her lovely shoulders before it caressed her all the way down to skim her knees. Her figure was showcased by the gown, shapely and feminine. He felt a tug of desire which surprised him. It wouldn't do to forget for a single moment she was an emissary from his grandfather.

Her hair was almost glowing, that beautiful burnished auburn displaying glittering golden threads. The bib necklace of diamonds and sapphires she wore would have put him through college. The dangling earrings in her ears caught and reflected the light. She was beautiful.

And dangerous. More men than he cared to remember

had met their fate entranced by beauty. He needed to keep a cool head around the woman.

Maybe it had been a mistake to dress as casually as he had, but he didn't like snobs and he had the feeling Clarissa was a first-class one. The jeans he wore were clean, but beginning to fade. Not worn, precisely, but not a fresh, dark blue anymore. He wore no tie with his white shirt, but had worn a sports jacket.

She looked stunning, he looked like a peasant. How would she react?

He stepped forward to find out.

"You look lovely," he said as way of greeting.

She turned and smiled politely, her expression giving nothing away. Jake knew she had to be dismayed to find him dressed as casually as he was. Still, he gave her credit for not letting it show. Strong breeding in Mademoiselle Clarissa Dubonette.

"You do me a great honor by having dinner with me," she said graciously. "I reserved a table for us in the main restaurant. I hope that's acceptable."

"Sounds good to me. Let's go."

By the time they were seated, Jake had reassessed his companion. Maybe she wasn't a snob. Maybe she was as gracious and sophisticated as she appeared. Her manners were excellent. She never let on if she felt a second's awkwardness. And she ignored the stares of the other diners when he'd followed her into the crowded restaurant.

He just hoped he didn't see anyone he knew. He'd never live it down—dressing like this for as fine a restaurant as she'd chosen.

As the evening progressed, he regretted deliberately trying to insult her by his attire. She seemed to be a nice woman, genuinely interested in all she'd seen in Los Angeles. The many questions she asked kept the conversation going until the meal was served.

"I need to talk to you about my reason for coming to Los Angeles," she said once the waiter had been assured they had everything they needed.

Jake felt himself tighten, felt the familiar anger flare. An instinctive reaction whenever he thought about his grandfather. The old wounds went deep.

"It's your dime."

"What?"

"An American expression. You're paying for dinner, you get to call the shots."

"Mmm." She studied him, her eyes dancing. "Excuse me, but this is an unusual situation for me. In our country, the royal family makes the rules. Since I'm dining with the heir to the throne, I'm almost at a loss."

"Doesn't seem like it to me." He wished she'd stop referring to his being the heir to the throne. A man ignored for his entire life couldn't become the king of a country he'd never seen.

She took a deep breath and put down her fork. "Crown Prince Michael and his son Philippe died a year ago in a motorboat accident. As you can imagine, the king was devastated. Actually—" her gaze dropped to her plate "—we all were." She was silent a moment, then looked up.

Jake watched her steadily. He could see the pain in her eyes. Had he heard his uncle and cousin had died?

He didn't remember. Of course having his father disinherited, and all ties to family cut before he was born, he had no reason to keep up with events halfway round the world or with people he had never met.

"By law and custom, the next in line to the throne is you. The king would like you to come to Marique to take your rightful place."

Jake gave her a sardonic smile. "Right. If he's so anxious to have me, why wait a year? And why did he send you instead of contacting me directly?"

"That would have been difficult. It would be awkward to contact you via phone or mail. Visiting royalty to your country must go through your Department of State—for security reasons. So there would have been no way he could have come quietly, spoken to you without the entire country and the world's press knowing what was going on. He prefers a more private solution. So he asked me to come in his stead."

"And what relationship do you have to the king?"

She peered at him, frowning. "I'm a close family associate, I suppose you could say. I speak English, know the family well, and can answer all your questions."

"That's why he sent you?"

She nodded. "That and I'd cause less comment than someone known to be a member of the royal family. Do you speak French?"

He shook his head. "Spanish. There are a lot of Mexican workers around here, it helps to speak their language. English must be spoken in Marique. Your command of it is excellent."

"I studied in England. Many of our citizens speak

some English, especially the younger ones, but not all. A major portion of the population also speaks Spanish. But French is our mother tongue.'' She smiled at him. ''Maybe your learning Spanish was prophetic.''

''Doubt it. It's handy here, as I said.''

''You'll be able to use it in Marique.''

''If I were going, which I'm not.''

Clarissa was growing frustrated. She didn't have a clue how to convince this man that he should at least *visit* Marique. Meet his grandfather, see what it would be like to be a king of a small country. In her opinion, it would be much better than working on a construction site in the hot sun!

''I can understand how you feel,'' she began.

''Can you? Did your father die when you were a baby?''

''No, he's still alive and in good health.''

''Did his parents cut you and your family off without a dime—even when you needed it desperately?''

She shook her head, dismay beginning to grow. She should not have tried that tactic. But she was desperate to find some connection, some way to reach him, to get him to agree to at least a visit. She couldn't tell the king she'd failed.

''Then don't tell me you *know* how I feel. You don't have a clue.''

That much was growing obvious. ''I stand corrected. I can only *imagine* how you might feel. But think for a minute what this could mean for you. Surely it would be better to rule a country than to swing a hammer all day? Instead of driving an older vehicle, you'd have enough money to buy whatever car you might wish. Instead of living alone in California, you'd be surrounded by family.''

She glanced at his jacket but kept her mouth shut. The outfit he was wearing was probably the best he owned. Why couldn't he see the advantages of what she was offering?

''And what would I have to do for all that? Nothing comes for free.''

Brightening, she smiled. Maybe that was the tack to take. ''Come to visit. The king is prepared to make you an allowance. Teach you how to handle the reins of government, impart all our history, and make you welcomed as the new heir.''

''Make me welcomed? After ignoring me for thirty-two years?''

Her smile faltered slightly, but she was making headway, she just knew it. She forged on—time to heal the breach. ''There will be an investiture ceremony once you're ready—crowning you as prince. The natural order of succession would then be assured.''

''What happens if I don't come?''

Clarissa didn't even want to think about that. What would happen if Jean-Antoine refused the crown? There had to be a contingency for that, though never in their six-hundred-year history had it happened.

''If you don't come to visit, then I will have failed in my mission. But I don't think I'll be the only one sent to convince you to come to Marique. I'm sure the king will send a minister next, or perhaps come himself even at the cost of publicity.''

"Which would reflect badly on him." Jake tried to picture an entourage hounded by the media while he tried to work. He looked at Clarissa. "Would you cut off your younger son because he tried to live his own life his way?"

"I'm not married, nor likely to be. I have no children, so I can't really answer. But I don't think so. I don't know the full story, however, so how can I say?"

"Why not?"

"Why not what?"

"Why are you not likely to be married?"

The old ache rose. It had been a year. Surely she should be over the pain by now.

"I was engaged to Philippe—your cousin. He died with his father. I doubt I'll find another love like we had in this life."

"Is that what this is about? Hang around me long enough and maybe you'll make crown princess after all?"

Clarissa felt the color drain from her face. She couldn't speak for the outrage that washed through her. Did he think she'd been engaged to Philippe *for the title?* How dare he! Good manners dictated she turn aside the insult. Her emotions didn't allow room for good manners, they threatened to swamp her where she sat.

She rose, took her handbag and walked from the restaurant without a word, head held high. She didn't trust herself not to scream at him! Tears shimmered in her eyes. No matter what the king had thought, she was not the person to talk his grandson into returning. Tonight proved that. The entire day proved it. And she was smart enough to know when to give up.

She'd call Marique in the morning and let His Majesty know she'd failed. With any luck, she could get on a flight to Paris before noon.

And never again would she try to be nice to Jean-Antoine. The man could fall off a beam and crack his skull for all she cared. Let him spend his entire life working in the blazing sun or the pouring rain and never learn a single solitary thing about his father's country. Let him do without family and history and tradition.

"Clarissa, wait!" he called after her.

She quickened her pace until she reached the lift. Pushing the call button repeatedly, almost frantically, she willed the doors to open. Quickly. She didn't want to be here—

"Clarissa, I'm sorry."

He stood beside her. She refused to look at him, blinking to keep the tears from falling, her gaze firmly on the lift doors. *Why didn't they open?*

"That was uncalled for and tactless and cruel. I apologize. I didn't mean it," Jake said in a low voice.

She yearned for the sanctity of her room. Emissary work was not for her. If anyone ever suggested it again, she'd—

"Clarissa, please say something. I'd take back the words in a heartbeat, if I could. I didn't mean to hurt you."

"You've made your position clear. There is nothing further to discuss. I'll inform the king in the morning of your decision." She refused to look at him.

He touched her shoulder and she shrank away. She didn't want to have anything to do with the man. He was nothing like his cousin. Breeding might tell, but so did schooling and polish and manners. He had all the couth of a lout. Did a lout have couth? Rough around the edges didn't begin to cover it. And so she'd tell the king. He had no idea what this man was like. She didn't want him to govern her country ever!

"Actually, if you'll forgive me for my hasty words, I'll come to Marique," Jake said just as the lift doors slid open. "Maybe it's time I told my grandfather exactly what I think of him and his treatment of my side of the family!"

CHAPTER TWO

CLARISSA hung up the phone the next morning feeling a bit uneasy. She'd spoken directly with the king, informing him that she and His Royal Highness would be arriving in a few days. But she wasn't optimistic about the outcome of the visit.

Jake had insisted he needed some time to arrange a leave at work before he could take off for a couple of weeks to visit Marique. What that encompassed, she had no idea. Couldn't he just tell the foreman he was leaving? Of course, that might get him fired, but he had an entire kingdom waiting for him, he didn't need some carpenter's job.

He remained insistent that the visit was only that—a short trip with no commitment on his part. He refused to even discuss moving there.

Clarissa took a deep breath. She wasn't going to worry about it. That was the king's domain. Her job was to get his grandson to return to Marique. She wasn't going to question closely why Jake had changed his mind. The anger that had shown in his expression last night gave her a clue. But she ignored it. He was coming. Her assignment was a success. End of story.

She had something more important to deal with—to decide how to cope with her roiling emotions if she was going to be around Jake for any length of time until they reached Marique. Brash and arrogant, he had spoken last night without thought. The words had still hurt.

She *had* loved Philippe. Had mourned his dying. And it had nothing to do with becoming a princess. Stupid male. Did they see everything as something to be gained or won?

Restless with inactivity, she rambled around the sitting room of her suite. She had nothing to do until dinnertime. She was meeting Jake again, ostensibly to discuss plans for their trip. She had two open-ended tickets to Paris. Once they reached France, they would change to the royal jetliner and fly home from there.

She felt there was little to discuss, but Jake had insisted he take her to dinner tonight. For a second Clarissa couldn't help the anticipation that rose at the thought. Last night's dinner had ended inauspiciously. She hoped tonight's would fare better.

Her anticipation was tinged with guilt. It wasn't that she was looking forward to seeing Jake precisely. It was more a hope to resolve all issues and set a day to return home.

Gazing out of her hotel window at the unfamiliar high-rise buildings of Los Angeles, she remembered every moment spent with Jake. She'd never before experienced such a hot reaction as she had when seeing his chest, muscular and gleaming in the hot sun. Clenching her hands into tight fists, she tried to ignore the yearning that still lingered to touch that warm skin, test the strength of those muscles.

She tried to ignore the feminine awareness that flooded when his gaze had roamed over her sending tendrils of heightened need shooting through. He was a man she'd just met. So he was a good-looking man. She had seen a hundred or more in her life.

But none that made her feel so delightfully feminine, a voice inside whispered. Or made her so conscious of being a woman, of longing for more from a man than words.

Blast it, she needed to think about something else!

Jean-Antoine, Jake as he was called here, deserved her loyalty and respect as future ruler of her country. Her entire family had always been loyal to the royal family. Clarissa was honored to have been sent as emissary and would do all she could to help in the transition if the king requested her assistance. But that definitely did not include fantasies about the sexiest man she'd ever seen!

What if they'd met under other circumstances? Despite her words to the contrary, she let her imagination soar.

The phone rang. Clarissa quickly crossed the room to answer, embarrassed by her train of thought.

"Hello?"

"Clarissa, Jake here."

"Yes, Your Highness."

There was a moment of silence. She could hear the background noise at the construction site.

"Jake. Call me Jake."

"I'm not sure that's proper." She had carefully refrained from calling him anything last night. Somehow his casual attire hadn't seem appropriate to his station, yet she couldn't be as informal as to call him Jake.

"Hey, if a prince can't order people to call him what he wants what's the good of being a prince?"

It was her turn to be silent. Then she slowly smiled. "Very well, *Jake*. Your wish is my command."

"I might like this arrangement. About supper. Wear jeans. I'll pick you up at six. We'll take my wheels tonight."

She pictured the battered truck he'd indicated yesterday. She wondered what held it together. Taking a breath she tried to infuse her voice with enthusiasm. "Very well. I don't have any jeans, however. Will a casual dress do?" She tried to remember the clothes she'd brought. She had not planned to stay beyond a couple of days, so had packed lightly.

"Didn't pack for California, huh? We're more casual here than most places. Jeans go anywhere."

"Actually, I don't have any jeans, here or at home."

"Then go get some today. You'll need them. Gotta go. Six."

She hung up, feeling dazed at the whirlwind conversation. He apparently planned to play this situation any way he wanted. First he wanted nothing to do with being a prince, then blatantly used his authority to get his own way. She thought the king was going to get more than he expected when Jake showed up.

She bit her lip in indecision. Should she discuss the visit with Jake? He wasn't planning to do anything to upset the king, was he? He'd said he just wanted to tell the king how he felt. She didn't fully trust him. Was that all he planned? Once he got that off his chest, would he settle in and learn what he needed to become king?

*   *   *

Promptly at the designated time, Clarissa stepped from the lift, feeling self-conscious and conspicuous. The jeans the saleswoman had assured her looked perfect were skintight. While they were comfortable, she was not certain that revealing every curve and valley to all and sundry was something she wanted.

Two men looked at her appreciatively. A small bump of feminine pleasure nudged her. Maybe it wasn't all bad after all. Her confidence rose slightly.

She'd given in to the saleswoman's blandishments and bought a short-sleeved, cotton sweater in bright yellow. It felt odd to wear such a cheerful color after a year of wearing somber clothing. But the official mourning time was past. Anyway, she didn't need to wear a specific color to mourn Philippe. She would always miss him.

And tonight, for some curious reason, she didn't wish to wear dark colors to dinner with Jake.

He was waiting near the lifts, casually dressed in the ubiquitous jeans and a polo shirt which displayed his physique perfectly—from his broad shoulders and muscular arms, to the flat belly and long legs. Glancing to meet his gaze, her heart jumped. God, she'd forgotten how gorgeous he was. Her heart fluttered and her stomach felt as if it had dropped ten stories.

Jake looked her up and down, his eyes glittering with male appreciation. "You look good enough to eat. Jeans suit you."

"Maybe." She refused to share her uncertainty. Let him think she was used to this.

"Ready to go?"

"As I'll ever be." She felt as if she were stepping out into the unknown, not just going to dinner.

It felt odd to be with the man, knowing one day he might rule her country. She found it too difficult to reconcile that idea. He walked with a sensuous grace that had her thinking licentious thoughts instead of focusing on the business at hand. He would tower over the others in the family, and his height had her feeling petite and feminine. The way he had of staring at a woman, brought every cell to attention, and made her angry at the same time. She wasn't something to ogle, she was on a mission! Yet he'd never done or said anything amiss. It was all in *her* mind.

She longed to dash away, back to the safety of her suite, yet kept walking beside him, her heart pounding, her expression as serene as she could force it.

They walked out into the late-afternoon sunshine. Glancing around, Clarissa didn't see the battered pickup truck. Probably the hotel doorman had asked him to park it out of sight.

He touched her shoulder and pointed to her left. She looked in that direction, conscious of his touch, of the heat that penetrated her sweater, of the fluttering sensations that tingled from her shoulder. He'd touched her more in the last two days than anyone had in a year. Casual touches that probably meant nothing to him. So why did she feel them to her toes?

In solitary splendor, a gleaming motorcycle sat at the curb, two black helmets dangling from the handlebars.

"That's your transportation?" she asked, astonished.

It was worse than the battered truck. A motorcycle? He expected her to ride on that? Was he crazy?

"Ever ridden one?"

She shook her head, staring at it in horror.

"It doesn't look safe. Where's your truck? I can call for the limousine driver. Or we can eat here," she said, scrambling around in her mind for other ideas. There had to be an alternative to a death-defying ride on a motorcycle.

Jake shrugged. "This'll be more fun. You're safe with me. I've had it a long time and no falls."

"Great. There's always a first time."

She'd seen the Southern California traffic yesterday when her chauffeur had maneuvered the limousine through the jammed-packed lanes, barreling along at incredible speeds. Now Jake proposed to propel them through that with nothing surrounding them but air?

"There may be a first time, but it's not tonight. Come on." He urged her over to the machine, reached out to take one of the helmets, which he handed her. Slipping the second one on his head, he watched her.

Clarissa pulled it on, feeling it close off some of the street noise. She tugged on the strap, trying to figure out how it fastened while her mind scrambled for a reason to stay here. Life and limb came to mind.

Jake brushed aside her hands and quickly snapped it closed. He turned and straddled the machine, then looked over his shoulder at her. "Climb on."

She stared at him and then at the minuscule space behind him on the seat. She would be plastered against him if she had to fit in that tiny space. Yet there was nowhere else.

"Maybe this isn't a good idea." No maybe about it, it definitely wasn't a good idea. How did one turn down the future ruler of her country?

"Come on, we're going to the beach. You'll love it."

Another sea enthusiast? Philippe had loved the water—odd she'd always thought, coming as he had from a land-locked country.

Resigned, she gingerly swung her leg over and settled in the leather seat. Its natural slant pushed her toward Jake despite her efforts to maintain a respectable distance.

"Hold me around my waist and lean with me when we turn," he said over his shoulder.

She swallowed and moved closer until her legs brushed against his, her thighs against the back of his, her feet finding the footrests. Her heart skipped a beat as she slowly encircled his waist with her arms, almost holding her breath as she hugged him. There was just no way to keep a respectable distance on this thing.

He was larger than she'd expected, her arms stretching to meet in front. She felt the iron-hard muscles of his abdomen as he kicked the machine into starting. His warmth was unsettling. Her heart began a rapid tattoo. When she took a breath, she could feel her breasts push against his back. His scent surrounded her, musky and electrifying. She tried to shrink away, but was too fearful of letting go. She knew he'd be dangerous, she needed to muster some defense.

Without a word, he put the bike into gear and roared

down the curving drive of the hotel, blending smoothly into the heavy flow of traffic. Instinctively, Clarissa tightened her grip. She was clinging like a limpet to Prince Jean-Antoine Simon Hercules LeBlanc! What would her mother think if she could see her?

She dare not even think of the king's reaction.

They wove through the traffic, heading west toward the late-afternoon sun. Once her initial fear faded, Clarissa began to enjoy herself. The air whipped against her skin, warm and dry. The feeling of speed was intensified with nothing surrounding her but the wind. She leaned with Jake when making turns, growing exhilarated as he swooped and dodged through the traffic. Who would have suspected what fun this could be?

She smelled the sea before it came into view. The air was cleaner, felt cooler. When Jake turned left onto a boulevard, she saw the ocean on their right, glittering in the late-afternoon sunshine. They rode parallel to it for a long time. Finally he pulled into a graveled lot right on the water.

He parked, cut the engine and took off his helmet. Looking over his shoulder, his eyes met hers and he grinned.

"Did you like it?"

She nodded slowly, trying to unfasten her fingers. She'd been gripping her hands so tightly she could scarcely let go. When she pulled her arms away, he got off the bike, hanging the helmet on the handlebar.

Clarissa stood, took off her helmet and shook her head, loosening her squashed-down hair. She glanced around. Except for a shack to the left, which seemed to be surrounded by surfboards and a dozen or so cars, she didn't see much but the beach.

"Is dinner a picnic?"

"No. That place has the best seafood at the beach." He gestured to the shack.

Clarissa refused to let her dismay show. They would have been better off dining at the hotel again.

Suddenly a thought struck. Maybe this was all Jake could afford. She felt badly if that was the case. He should have been brought to the palace when his father died, raised there, rather than abandoned by his grandparents and left alone to fend for himself in America.

For the first time, Clarissa questioned if the king had made the right decision thirty-some years ago.

The shack had few tables inside, more located on a large deck on the far side. Jake led them directly to a table on the edge of the deck that commanded a spectacular view of the Pacific.

"The Captain's Platter is the best thing on the menu, but order anything you want," he said when she sat down, handing her a menu from the rack at the side of the table.

Clarissa looked at the offerings, all seafood, from prawns and popcorn shrimp, to clams, oysters and the fresh-catch-of-the-day. She also glanced at the prices, and quickly calculated the conversion. An inexpensive place to dine.

For a moment a pang struck her anew. She kept her gaze fastened on the menu, lest Jake suspect. He'd mentioned how hard he and his mother had things. He drove a motorcycle instead of a car. And now he brought her to an inexpensive restaurant.

Things were going to be so different for him once he assumed his rightful role. It was a shame the king had not done right by this grandson from the beginning. It was hardly Jake's fault his father had not pleased the king.

"I'll have the Captain's Platter, then," she said.

"My wish is your command?" he asked, raising an eyebrow.

She looked up at that. "Actually, it looks good and offers a sample of everything."

His dark eyes studied her and Clarissa wanted to scream to him to stop it. Could he see the heat rising in her cheeks? Notice the increased beat of her pulse? Realize every cell throbbed with renewed life? Flustered, she dragged her gaze away, staring at the ocean and the sun slowly sinking toward the horizon. What was the matter with her?

When the orders had been placed, with a waiter who looked as if he'd just come in from surfing the waves, Clarissa bravely looked back at Jake.

"Did you sort it all out at work? Are you ready now to fly to Marique?" She could do this—by keeping everything on a strictly business level!

"I will be day after tomorrow."

"Did you have to quit?"

He shook his head, narrowing his eyes a bit. "What do you know about my job?"

"Only what the king told me. Apparently he had a report from a detective some years ago that you were working for a construction firm. I believe you are a carpenter?''

"Among other things. I can do a bit of all building aspects, except plumbing. Never got interested in that beyond the basics. How long ago was the report made?''

"I don't know, maybe when you turned twenty-one. Does it matter?''

"No. It explains things, though.''

"What things?''

"Never mind. Tell me more about Philippe.''

She blinked. "Don't you want to know about your grandfather, or Marique?''

"We'll get to those. I want to know about your fiancé.''

"Why?''

"He was my cousin, wasn't he?''

Clarissa wondered what exactly Jake wanted. Why talk about someone who was no longer there?

"He wasn't as tall as you, but had the same dark hair and eyes. He loved sports—polo and skiing and boat racing. That's what killed him, a failure on a new powerboat he was trying out. He and his father had gone together for a shakedown run. The speedboat didn't make one of the turns, but flipped over going about a hundred miles an hour, crashing down on them both.'' She stopped. Even now, thinking about it brought an ache to her heart.

"What a waste.''

"It was. And over something so foolish as racing,'' she said with some asperity.

"My father died in a race car accident.''

"All you LeBlanc men must love speed, look at our ride here."

He shook his head. "We never once exceeded the speed limit. I do like the feeling of freedom when riding the bike, but I'm not after speed for speed's sake. What did my cousin do when he wasn't off skiing or playing polo or racing? Did he have a job?"

"He considered himself a goodwill ambassador. He loved to travel, up to Paris, or over to Geneva. Italy was a favorite spot."

"Did you go with him?"

"Occasionally to Paris, when my mother or aunt could chaperone."

He narrowed his gaze again. "Chaperone? I thought you said you two were engaged."

"We were. All the more reason to have a chaperone."

He said nothing. Just then the waiter brought their platters, piled high with a dozen varieties of seafood and crisp fries.

"What did he do for a living? I assume he had some responsibilities around the place."

"Not many. His father was crowned prince. He had more to do, as much as the king would delegate. But Philippe was content with being a goodwill ambassador. Once his father assumed the throne, his training would have intensified to fit him for the future role of king."

"So he was off flitting around, leaving you home alone. Doesn't sound like much of a life."

Clarissa took offense. "It was fine. Things would have changed once we were married."

"How?"

She hesitated. She had hoped things would change, but had no real reason beyond her own wishes that Philippe would have stayed home more once they married. "He would have had a wife and home of his own."

Jake shrugged. "Tell me about Marique."

"Do you know anything about the country?"

"It's small, about the size of one of our smaller states. Located near Liechtenstein, in the Pyrenees mountains between France and Spain. Beyond that, not much. What's the economy like?"

"Struggling," she said after a moment's pause. There was no use whitewashing things, he'd see himself soon enough.

"Why?"

Loyalty guarded her tongue. She tried to think up a way to present the situation while still painting the king in a favorable manner.

Jake would have none of it. "Just say it. It won't go beyond this table."

"Your grandfather is eighty-four. His sights seemed still on the way things were done when he was younger. Wool exports used to be our moneymaker. But with the rise of synthetic fabrics, that market has declined in recent years."

"The country is located in some prime real estate. No ski resorts, spas, something to lure tourists?"

"We have one ski place, but nothing elaborate. Nothing to compare with Gstaad, for instance. Or your American resorts. At least that's what Philippe said. He tried them all. He liked going to Switzerland and America."

"That's what Philippe said—you never went?"

She shook her head, reluctant to admit the fact. She had recognized the restlessness in her fiancé, never liked it, but had accepted it long ago.

"What do you do in Marique? Or don't you have a job, either?"

Clarissa put down her fork. The food was excellent, just as Jake had declared. But she was already growing full and only half the plate was empty. She glanced at his plate. He obviously had a big appetite, as he didn't appear to be slowing down at all.

"I work for Ambere Soaps."

"Soaps?"

"There is a village about thirty kilometers from the capital which produces fine soaps. It's mostly a cottage industry, women make the soaps to earn extra money since the sheep industry has declined. I work with them in marketing and exportation of products. It's an excellent beauty product and I hope the small industry can expand."

"Would you have continued working after your marriage?"

"Probably not."

"When was the big day?"

"We hadn't set a date. Don't you want to learn more about your grandfather?" She didn't like talking about her past. Especially when she'd been upset enough with Philippe for not setting a date.

Jake shook his head. "I know all I need to know. He is more focused on ritual and duty than family loyalty. He turned his back on one son because he didn't do exactly what his father thought he should. He refused any aid to his daughter-in-law, even in dire circumstances. And he totally ignored this grandson until nothing remained but duty to contact that same grandson in hopes of continuing the family dynasty. He's left it too late. Did I leave anything out?''

Clarissa remained silent. It wasn't her place to criticize the royal family. But the anger in Jake's tone clearly told her how he felt about the situation. Did he transfer those feelings to her as the messenger?

The thought surprised her. Why should she care? She wasn't here to become friends with this man.

No matter how much he intrigued her.

''Then why are you going to visit?'' she asked.

Jake leaned back in his chair and looked out to the ocean. The gentle breeze that swept in cooled things down, and carried a hint of the sea. When he glanced at Clarissa, she solemnly watched him. Waiting for what? What did she expect—for him to confess he planned to go for revenge? To make his grandfather think he was considering staying, then let him know in no uncertain terms what he could do with his family loyalty and dynastic tradition?

It was obvious she thought he should be dancing in joy at the summons from his grandfather.

He narrowed his gaze against the setting sun's glare. He could still back out but honesty had him admitting his curiosity. He wondered what his father's father was like. What the country was like that couldn't hold the men. First his father had left to find adventure, then his cousin and uncle.

Did the king rule with ruthlessness? Did he refuse to relinquish any meaningful duties to his family so they needed to seek life satisfaction elsewhere? Or was it just too boring to tolerate?

"When will you be ready to go?" Clarissa asked.

The sun's sheen on her auburn hair highlighted the glints of gold. It looked silky and hot. He had a sudden yearning to thread his fingers through, to feel the softness, see if it captured the warmth from the sun, or was as cool as the sea.

His gaze moved to her mouth, with her red lips dampened from her tongue. Would she be polite and placid if he kissed her, or hot and fiery to match her hair?

She wasn't his usual style, but the interest was there. Was it one-sided?

He usually didn't have much to do with women unless they knew the score. He'd been focused for years on buying his way into the company, then building it to the next stage. There would be plenty of time later to look for a mate once he'd achieved his other goals. In the meantime, he wasn't against a dalliance from time to time.

He still had a feeling Clarissa was definitely off-limits. But it wouldn't hurt to test the waters.

"Want to go back to your place, or mine?" he asked, leaning closer, running a fingertip down her arm.

She sat up at that, her eyes wide with shock as she yanked her arm away. "I *meant* to Marique. How long does it take to tell the foreman of the job you are leaving?"

"I don't want to leave him in the lurch." It rankled

that his grandfather apparently thought him nothing more than a carpenter. Not that there would be anything wrong with that if it was his chosen profession. He'd started out that way and still loved working with wood. But that had been a long time ago. Now he was the majority partner in the construction firm. They'd recently successfully expanded from specializing in building luxury homes to include small shopping malls and government buildings.

He rarely got the chance to swing a hammer anymore. He was lucky if he got one or two days on a job site each quarter.

His days recently had been yesterday and that morning.

He almost smiled at the thought of going to Marique as a carpenter. He could wear jeans, leave the suits at home. Bumble around, reinforcing all the concepts his grandfather obviously held. Maybe offer to help with repairs around the family castle. Would the old man have apoplexy at the thought of a prince fixing a wobbly railing?

Meeting Clarissa's clear, candid gaze, however, he reconsidered. Deceit didn't sit well with him, for whatever reason. And it was unfair to others to perpetuate the myth for the sake of annoying his grandfather—much as he might wish to.

"There's a bit more involved than just telling a foreman I'm going. I run the firm. I'm having my assistant rearrange things, delegate assignments and projects to managers, and I'm trying to bring everyone up to speed so they can deal with critical situations in order to take a couple or three weeks to visit Marique.''

Clarissa stared at him in disbelief. ''You own the construction firm?'' She frowned in suspicion. ''I thought you were a worker. Nothing in my briefing said anything about owning the company.''

''Well, your information is out of date. I'm the majority stockholder. There're others involved, as well.''

''But you run it? What were you doing yesterday at that construction site?''

''I started as a carpenter back when I was in college. I still like the work—visiting sites when I get the chance.''

''You've attended college?'' she asked. Her disbelief was almost comical, but Jake wasn't amused by her incredulity and almost swore in frustration.

''U.C.L.A. M.B.A.'' he snapped.

''Is that a code?''

''I attended the University of California at Los Angeles and ended up with a Masters in Business Administration. It's a graduate degree.''

He had to give her credit, in the blink of an eye, her expression smoothed out, and she regained control of her astonishment. She had that professional persona down pat.

''I guess my grandfather doesn't know all that?'' he asked sardonically.

''I don't think so. He hired that private investigator some time ago. I don't know how much has been updated over the years.''

''There was no need before now,'' he said. It irked

him—knowing that as long as his grandfather had his oldest son and other grandson, he had no use for him. Now there was no one else left. But his uncle and cousin had died more than a year ago. Why wait until now to contact him?

"I'll be ready to go on Thursday. Will that suit?"

"Yes. I'll make the arrangements."

"Do me a favor."

Clarissa looked at him warily. "If I can."

"Don't tell my grandfather what I just told you. I'll let him know in my own time."

She hesitated a moment. "I won't lie if he asks."

"I doubt he will. Just don't volunteer."

She nodded, suddenly realizing how convoluted palace intrigues could become. "Very well."

"Are you finished?"

She looked around, surprised to find she was sorry the evening was ending.

"Want to ride along the beach for a while? It's not even dark yet," he asked.

"On the bike?"

"Live dangerously."

"That's my new motto."

"What was your old one?"

"I don't think I had one. Maybe you're rubbing off on me."

"I don't live dangerously."

"What do you call tearing along on a motorcycle in the infamous Los Angeles traffic? Or walking a high beam on a construction site with no safety net."

He laughed. "Construction sites don't have safety nets."

"I know. I believe that was my point." She swallowed hard. When he smiled, he was undoubtedly the most gorgeous man she'd ever seen. Her heart fluttered again, and once more she wondered what she'd be unleashing on the women in Marique when she arrived with the prince.

"Walking the high beams isn't that dangerous. That just adds a bit of spice to life. Dangerous would be falling for a woman like you."

CHAPTER THREE

DANGEROUS would be falling for a woman like you. Two days later as they boarded the jet for Paris, Clarissa heard the echo of the words Jake had spoken at the shanty restaurant for about the millionth time. She hadn't seen Jake since he'd returned her to her hotel Tuesday night. But that hadn't stopped her from thinking about him. And remembering.

Clarissa alternated from indignation that he'd ever suggest such a thing, and fear that she'd almost like to explore that possibility.

Not that she wanted anything more to do with men—especially LeBlanc men. She'd loved Philippe. She missed him dreadfully and never wanted to risk her heart a second time. She still remembered the shock she'd felt when told of his death. The feeling of her life ending. The days in a daze as she came to terms with the changes life would forever hold. She dare not risk that hurt again.

Especially with someone like Jake.

She didn't trust him to do right by his family. Didn't trust him to behave—around the king or around her. He had that don't-give-a-damn way about him that secretly thrilled her at the same time it annoyed her to bits.

She liked her men suave, debonair, polite and smooth. Not earthy, sexy, sardonic and annoying.

She tried to remind herself that he'd fought his way out of that poor neighborhood in Las Vegas—gaining

46

the respect of others as he moved up. But she didn't believe that he'd fit in once he reached Marique. He didn't have decades of training behind him. Didn't understand the nuances or infrastructure of the country's politics or international protocols. He didn't even know his grandfather's name besides King Guilliam!

And he certainly was not going with the proper deference and respect she thought he should have. That chip on his shoulder hadn't budged with regard to his grandfather.

As the plane taxied away from the airport, Jake realized he was committed to visiting his only living relative despite vowing to never do so. Before the visit ended, Jake planned to unload a few home truths. His grandfather had had no use for him for thirty-some years, Jake had no use for him now.

In the meantime, he settled into the first-class accommodations and remembered Clarissa's narrowed gaze when he had arrived in his suit. He knew by her expression she was remembering their first dinner together. The owner of a successful construction firm obviously had better clothes than he'd worn. Would she comment on his lapse?

Gracious as ever, she had not said a word.

He studied her somber attire, remembering the tight jeans and bright sweater she'd worn Tuesday night. Remembering how the sun had shone on her hair, picking out the golden highlights. How her enthusiasm for commonplace things intrigued him—so different from her formal demeanor when she was fully conscious of whom she represented. He especially liked how her eyes had sparkled when they forgot to be sad. And how much her lips enticed.

He had no intentions of falling for her or any other woman anytime soon. And certainly never for a woman from a world so different from his own. Raised in the aristocracy, her education, beliefs and standards were as different from his as night and day.

She remained fun to tease, however, and he had no intention of stopping.

"Do you spend a lot of time in court?" he asked Clarissa once she seemed settled in her seat and the plane was taxiing down the runway.

She looked puzzled. "I'm not a lawyer. I told you, I work in marketing."

"Court. Isn't that what they call it? Like the Court of St. James?"

She frowned. "I don't understand."

"At the palace, doing royal things."

Her laughter sparkled. "Doing royal things? What are royal things?"

He leaned closer, as if imparting a secret. Her light floral scent invaded. Taking a breath, he tried to ignore the thoughts that came instantly to mind—which had nothing to do with royalty. "Things royals do, I guess. Want to explain to me?"

She pulled back a bit, her eyes becoming wary. An interesting reaction, Jake thought.

"I don't have a formal position there, if that's what you mean. I did participate in official state functions when Philippe was alive, as his fiancée. Now, I doubt I'll be included."

"Did you enjoy it?"

"Some of it. Are you worried about what's involved?"

"Should I be? I'm simply coming to visit my grandfather."

"You're the heir to the throne, coming to meet his people," she corrected, eyeing him skeptically.

"Then I expect I'll need a guide to understand fully what is required. I'd hate to make a major faux pas on my initial visit."

"So there will be others?" She was quick to jump on his words.

"A lot depends on this visit, don't you think?" He had no intention of telling her his plans. Time enough for all to see.

"I'm sure the king has plans—"

"I'll choose you."

Clarissa looked at him in astonishment. "What? I can't be your guide!"

"Why not?"

"I'm sure the king has definite ideas and plans about what he wants you to see and do. And I would not be suitable to provide the instruction you'd need."

"We're not talking a lifetime commitment. I'm only going for two or three weeks."

"No."

"Then let's forget the whole thing. I'll visit Paris for a few days and then return home." He settled back in his seat, guessing which way Clarissa would respond.

"You said you'd come to Marique," she said in outrage. "You can't go back on your word!"

He almost smiled. She definitely should never play poker, she would lose her shirt.

"All right then, as prince of Marique, I command you to act as my guide while I'm visiting."

"You can't just order me to do whatever you want!"

For a moment another order sprang to mind. One involving dark rooms and closed doors and a wide bed. Too bad *droit du seigneur* had fallen from favor.

"I thought my wish was your command."

"You're enjoying this, aren't you?" she asked suspiciously.

"You bet. I haven't had such fun in years," he said. "Imagine having an entire nation at my beck and call."

"Good rulers lead, they do not exploit!"

"Ah, my first lesson? So how do I lead you into being my guide?"

"Your wish, of course, is my command," she said through gritted teeth, her eyes flashing. "Unless the king has other plans. He could countermand your orders. He is the ruler, not you."

Satisfied with her compliance, however reluctantly given, he changed to a serious note. "What are the contingency plans if he had no heir?"

"But he does. You."

Jake shook his head. After he finished with the old man, the last thing he would want was Jake to succeed him.

Clarissa reached out a hand and rested it on his arm, as if he might get up and walk away. "Please, Jake, give it an honest chance, won't you? It's a great little country, full of people going along, making a living, having families. Our monarchy has been going strong for six hundred years. At least go with an open mind, please?"

The plane had reached its cruising altitude. Jake settled back in his seat and loosened his seat belt. "That may be asking too much. Tell me about what you think I should know about you."

"Me? Don't you mean the country?"

"I can learn about that once I'm there. I'm curious about my new guide."

Clarissa glared at him despite feeling exhilarated. Sparring with the man would drive her crazy, but it was a good kind of crazy. An alive crazy. She felt as if she'd been drifting for far too long. She had no confidence the king would want her to spend a lot of time with Jake, but agreeing was easier than arguing the point.

And for a moment, she tried to envision what it would be like to try to show Jake around the country, share its history, customs and traditions. Would they have quiet little talks while walking in the gardens? Or would he want to see the countryside on a motorcycle, racing around corners and scaring half the population with his recklessness?

That wasn't fair, she thought. He hadn't been really reckless to her knowledge. It had been exciting riding with him on the freeways in California. But while she'd been thrilled, she also felt safe. He'd been in total control.

He obviously knew what he was doing in construction, he was still in perfect shape after having worked in the field for many years. Another area mastered.

He was in control now. Maybe she'd take this assignment to see what she could do to chip away some of that control.

"Know the opposition?" she asked lightly.

"Are we opposing forces? I'd rather think of us as allies, united for a common goal."

"And that goal being?"

"Harmony while I visit my grandfather."

"My goal is a bit more, I think."

"Don't, Clarissa. You'll be setting yourself up for failure. Tell me about yourself."

"Your wish is—"

"And if you say that again unless I specifically order you to do so, I'll take drastic measures."

"Like what?"

"Like banishing you to the far reaches of the country," he said whimsically.

"All that way?" She opened her eyes wide in mock fear. "How would I ever manage?"

"Or kiss you until you can't talk back."

His low voice washed through her like mulled wine, the words penetrating a second later. Heat suffused. Her gaze dropped to his lips and for a moment she half wished he would kiss her.

What was she thinking of? He had no business teasing her like that. *Dangerous would be falling for a woman like you.*

Her eyes flashed as she glared at him. "Your behavior leaves much to be desired!"

He laughed.

Incensed, Clarissa wanted to puncture that arrogance, to knock him down a peg or two. But words failed her.

She was further angered when he settled back in his chair and closed his eyes. Did he plan to ignore her and sleep the twelve hours it took to fly to Paris since she hadn't answered his question?

Seething in frustration, Clarissa studied him. She was ready to argue the point and he had his eyes closed as if he'd shut out everything. His dark hair was thick and trimmed. His skin was tanned from long hours in the sun. Even in the dark gray business suit he wore, his muscular frame was clear. This was not some dilettante who played at working. This was a man who built things, managed a large, successful, multilevel construction company.

She wondered if he would succumb to the allure of royalty, of the trappings of riches and change his mind once he saw the palace in Marique. Pride had its place, but not here. From the little she knew of him, he'd had a hard life. Surely being surrounded by affluence and the commanding life his grandfather offered would woo him away from Los Angeles.

Or would it? She suspected His Royal Highness was very much his own man. He had accomplished a great deal in thirty-two years. And most likely not by being nice.

How would he and the king react?

She didn't want to analyze her own reaction as the anger began to fade. Was he truly asleep, or merely ignoring her?

Her heart skipped a beat when she thought of his threat to kiss her. Here? On the plane? He wouldn't dare!

Not that she planned to put it to the test. Here or anywhere. But she couldn't help speculating how it would feel to have him take her in his arms and cover her mouth with his. Would he be a little rough given his upbringing? Or smooth and polished from practice over the years? Strong and demanding, or gentle and coaxing?

Hardly coaxing, she couldn't picture that at all. But she could imagine being swept away and becoming lost in the rapture of the moment.

She frowned as she turned to gaze out the window, trying to cool off. Just thinking about the man had her blood racing through her veins. Gorgeous as he was, he probably had women by the dozen lining up to spend time with him. Was she just one of many?

Or was he involved seriously with one?

Maybe he was married.

The information she'd been given made no mention of it either way. But the report was obviously years out of date since nothing of his connection to the construction firm had been noted.

"Now what?" he asked.

She looked at him in surprise. "I thought you were asleep."

"You were too quiet, that worried me. Don't ever play poker, Clarissa, your face is too expressive. Something's bothering you, what?"

"Are you married?"

He looked startled. "No. Not married, never have been."

"Why not? Aren't a lot of men married by your age?"

"Why aren't you married, aren't a lot of women married by your age?" he turned back.

"I told you I was engaged and he died."

"Otherwise you would have been married by now?"

She wanted to give an emphatic yes, but in all honesty she didn't know. They'd never set a date. Several times she'd brought up the subject, but Philippe had never wanted to commit to a date. Would they have been married by now? She liked to think so but honesty had her shrugging her shoulders.

"How old are you, Clarissa?"

"Twenty-seven."

"I'm thirty-two. You probably already knew that."

She nodded.

"I've been building my career, which was a lot more important than marriage. Hell, I don't know if I ever want to marry after seeing what kind of life my mother had after my father died. She was a small-town girl from Nebraska who moved seeking the glamorous life in Las Vegas. That's where they met. After a whirlwind courtship, they married. Both were young, immature and irresponsible, as far as I can tell. He left her with nothing, and she had no skills beyond dancing to support herself and a child. And the glamorous life in Vegas is like that of a model's. It isn't long before younger, prettier girls are getting all the choice spots."

"You don't plan to marry because of that?"

"That's a major factor."

"You could change things. Chances are you'll live a long life and not leave a young family behind. And even if you died young, you could make sure they were provided for. You're not as young as your father was when he died. And don't seem at all irresponsible." She had no trouble picturing him excelling in the romance department!

He shrugged. "What about you, willing to try again?"

She was silent for a moment. Did she want to fall in love again, risk her heart a second time? She didn't think so.

"I like my life the way it is now. I have friends, family and a job I love and find challenging."

"That's not answering the question."

"Then, no, I don't want to risk it again."

"So we have something in common."

"It's different for you, you have an obligation to marry."

"Obligation?"

"To insure the monarchy."

The momentary feeling of camaraderie evaporated. "I damn well do not. If I didn't want to marry before, I'm sure as hell not going to marry for some dynastic succession in a country I've never stepped foot in."

"But you'll be there soon. I predict you'll feel differently once there."

"And that is because?"

"You'll have more than you ever expected."

Jake wondered where this was leading. "Such as?"

"Family."

"Which I had until my mother died. I don't need a grandpa at this late date."

"Wealth."

"I have enough."

Jake was annoyed she thought the idea of wealth could sway his convictions. Was that what everyone thought—that he was the poor relation who would leap at the chance to inherit a kingdom?

How would this play out? Would it be in his best interests to see what enticements were offered before rejecting them all and returning home? Anger still burned whenever he remembered the cavalier treatment his grandfather had displayed toward his mother. Revenge would be sweet.

He just wished his mother was alive. She would have loved to visit Marique. Given the current circumstance, Jake could have given her anything she wanted. Timing was everything. In this case, the timing was way too late.

The long journey was made palatable by the in-flight movies, the first-class meals and the comfort of the seats. Jake was restless, nonetheless. He hated the inactivity of sitting for such a long time.

The change of planes in Paris was swift and without incident. Soon they were heading south over France on their way to Marique. The royal jet was much smaller than a commercial airliner, but spacious enough to move around in and be comfortable. Clarissa had handled everything, her French rapid and flawless. She insisted Jake sit by the window to better see Marique when they approached.

Once they reached Marique, she'd be more than a guide—she'd be a translator. Could he trust her? Or would her loyalty to the royal family color the translations of the conversations?

When they prepared to land, Jake settled by the window to study the terrain as they descended. Clarissa watched him, wondering how she would have felt coming to Marique for the first time as an adult.

She knew his bitterness ran deep. And she couldn't blame him. His childhood had been needlessly rough. But he had to put that behind him and stay. The stability of her small country depended on this one man.

She looked over his shoulder at the familiar mountains and valleys. A leap of joy made itself felt. She loved

Marique. Couldn't wait to see her parents, visit with her friends, see her nieces and nephew. It seemed more than a week had passed since she had left.

"It's pretty, don't you think?" she asked softly.

He looked at her over his shoulder, her head so close to his she could feel his breath skim across her cheeks. Clarissa pulled back a fraction, trying to hide how uncomfortable she felt so close to him. Her heart stuttered any time he came close. She felt as shy as a teenager with her first crush. What was the matter with her? She wasn't even sure she liked the man. But he sure made her body sit up and take notice. Goodness, she needed to practice some kind of distancing!

"Hard to tell much from the air. How far from the airport is the capital city?"

"About twenty minutes. The palace is there, too. Your family has a summer place beside an alpine lake to the west. But normally the family resides in the palace."

"Who's there now?"

"Your grandfather, of course. You know your grandmother died shortly after your father left home. The king has been alone a long time."

Jake merely raised an eyebrow at her attempt to gain some sympathy. Clarissa ignored him and continued, "Prince Michael and your aunt Gustine had apartments there. One of their daughters, Marie, lives with Gustine, the older one, Claudine, is married. Philippe also had an apartment in the palace."

"One big happy family," he said sardonically.

"Each had his own space. Sometimes they gathered together for meals, but rarely. Only for official state dinners did the entire family sit down together."

"My aunt stayed?"

"Why not? It is her home. She still lives in the quarters she and Crown Prince Michael occupied, with your cousin Marie. Claudine lives with her husband, of course."

"So there are others in line for the crown?"

Clarissa shook her head. "Succession goes through the males, not the females."

"Not very progressive."

Clarissa remained prudently silent.

"So, what do you think?" she asked as the limousine sent for them approached the palace sometime later. The soft pinkish tint to the stones that comprised the structure glowed in the afternoon sun. The ornate battlements and turrets always reminded her of fairy tales and romance. It was a fantastic building, with fancy sculptures and abutments that added romance to the soft color of the stone.

Immense wrought-iron gates stood wide. Slowly they drove up the drive, flanked on both sides by lovely gardens and pristine lawns neatly tended. Clarissa loved the place, not only for what it represented, but for the sheer beauty.

They stopped beside the front doors—huge structures more than fifteen feet tall which continued the ornate decorative theme from the gates, with dragons and mythical birds carved deep into the dark wood.

Clarissa wondered if the king was honoring his grandson with all the pomp at his command, or was he rather trying to intimidate him?

She suppressed a smile. She doubted anything would intimidate Jake White.

He hadn't said a word, but she could see he was taking in everything. When a liveried footman opened the door, she slid from the vehicle and waited for Jake. Despite his insistence she call him Jake, he was the prince and she deferred to him.

He stood on the steps and looked up, studying the structure for a long moment before looking at Clarissa. "Nice place. A bit pretentious, but it looks in good repair."

"It was built in the height of the romantic period. I've always loved it."

A distinguished man in military dress came to the door and spoke to Clarissa. He bowed slightly, spoke to Jake in French, then stood aside.

"We've been summoned. I thought we might go directly to the family quarters, but apparently the king wishes to meet you in one of the state rooms. They are very beautiful," she said softly.

Jake gave her a knowing look and Clarissa turned away to head for the door. He knew what the old man was about. It would prove enlightening to watch the two of them meet.

Clarissa introduced Jake to Minister du Rubine, noticing Jake wasn't intimidated by the general. She quickly translated between them, frustration growing. The general spoke English. Why was he pretending not to?

"We're to go to the Red Room. It's one of the most formal," she said as they followed the general. Jake was silent, but Clarissa felt the growing tension.

Uniformed footmen waited by the door to the Red

Room, opening them with a flourish. A six-foot-wide stretch of red carpeting ran down the long length of the room—directly to the ornately carved and gilded thrones at the far end. Except for the king, seated on one of the thrones, and one other man standing at his right, the room was empty.

"I should have worn jeans," Jake muttered for her ears only.

"No, you shouldn't have! You're perfect the way you are!" She glanced at him again. Despite traveling for more than twenty hours, he looked as fresh as when he'd arrived at the airport in Los Angeles. She felt rumpled next to him. But this meeting wasn't about her, it was for Jake and his grandfather.

He stepped forward and Clarissa remained where she was. If the king wished her to join them, he would summon her.

Jake hesitated and turned toward her. "Coming?"

She shook her head.

He reached out and captured her arm in a no-nonsense grip. "Oh, yes, you are. As my guide and translator, where I go, you go."

"The king speaks English, you don't need me."

"I suspect the general does, as well," he said knowingly, "but that doesn't mean he did. You come with me."

Clarissa dare not protest, but she felt uncomfortable. And aware of the man holding her, of the shimmering tension, nerves stretched tightly.

She wondered if she'd ever forget how the sensations spiraling through her charged her as if with electricity. She felt vibrant and exciting and for a moment, needed by this sexy man. Throwing aside caution, she walked beside him proudly.

The king stood when Jake reached the throne. He was tall despite his eighty-four years. His hair was receding slightly, silvery in color and worn short. His attire was European in style and he wore the expensive clothing with a casualness of long custom. His eyes were not as dark as Jake's, more a milk-chocolate brown. They were grave. No spark of warmth showed.

"Welcome to Marique," he said formally and in English. "It is time to take your rightful place in our country."

Jake inclined his head slightly in response. "I'm here for a visit, nothing more. We'll see how things shake out."

The king frowned and looked at Clarissa. "Did you not tell him of my expectations?"

"Yes, Your Majesty, I did."

The king glared at Jake. "I'd think a carpenter would jump at the chance of bettering himself."

Jake's grip tightened on Clarissa's arm when she instinctively began to correct the king's misunderstanding. She closed her mouth, remembering his request when they'd eaten dinner on the beach.

"There's nothing like swinging a hammer to keep a man going. Don't suppose there are any repair jobs you need done while I'm visiting?"

The king frowned and sat back in his chair, waving one hand. "Go. Show him to his rooms. He can meet the rest of the family at dinner."

He looked suddenly older, more subdued. Clarissa yanked her arm free from Jake's and turned, walking swiftly back down the long room, holding on to her anger by a thread.

He easily caught up with her in the hallway, spinning her around to face him.

"What are you hoping to gain by letting him continue to think you're a carpenter when we both know you run a huge company and have moved far beyond that? You could have been more polite, not baiting him!" she almost shouted. "He doesn't deserve your attitude. He's our king!"

"Oh and I deserve his? The most formal room in the place, probably. No warm welcome, no 'Hi, Grandson, nice to finally meet you!' Maybe I want a chance to have him find out more about me on his own, without an investigator or anyone else telling him everything about me. Did you ever think about that? See if he can bring himself to establish some kind of relationship—and not feel like the end result of a report!"

"And if he doesn't fall into your plans?"

"If he thinks I'm not worth getting to know, then I'll know where I stand. He's had things all his way for my entire life. Time I had a say," Jake said. "Now the question is, are you with me in this or with him?"

CHAPTER FOUR

BEFORE Clarissa could respond, Jake heard a throat being cleared. He spun around. Standing behind him was a liveried man of indeterminate age. He was gazing off into space, as if by not looking at Jake and Clarissa, he could pretend he was invisible.

"What do you want?" Jake snarled.

The man blinked and looked at Clarissa. She spoke swiftly in French and he answered in the same language.

"He's to show you to your quarters."

"Can't he tell when people are having a private conversation?"

"Since he doesn't speak English, it doesn't matter what we say, he won't understand. And he's one of the servants, it's not his place to listen."

"As if that would stop him." Some of the intensity of emotion began to fade. Jake had been up for more than twenty-four hours straight. Fatigue began to make itself felt now that the initial meeting with his grandfather had passed.

The man spoke again and Clarissa nodded.

"His instructions were to show you to your quarters once your meeting with the king was concluded." She glanced at her watch. "It's not even four o'clock. Dinner is at eight. You'd have time for a nap. I don't know about you, but I'm exhausted."

"Will you be here for dinner?"

"I have not been invited."

"Then consider this an invitation. Or royal command, whatever. I imagine tonight's dinner won't quite be like the one we had at the beach."

Clarissa inclined her head slightly. "I'll be here at eight."

Jake watched her walk quickly away, then turned to follow the uniformed servant. When they turned down a long corridor, his attention was caught by the endless row of portraits. The paintings were large, almost life-size. He slowed down to look more closely. Different eras were depicted. The style of gowns changed with each new woman's face. The men wore their hair long in one era, short in most. Some sported luxurious mustaches, others were clean shaven.

As he studied them, he began to recognize certain traits—like those he shared with his father. Dark eyes, strong jaw. Was height a common feature? It was hard to tell when they were seated, or standing alone in a portrait.

For the first time, Jake felt a hint of belonging. He was the end generation of a long family line. If he never married, had no children, this branch of the LcBlanc family name would end with him.

He almost sympathized with the king. It couldn't have been easy to see his son and grandson die and know his only hope of family continuity rested with an unknown stranger from a foreign land.

"Ici." The man stopped and opened the doors with a flourish. He stood aside, at attention while Jake stepped into the lavishly appointed sitting room. The tall windows on the outside wall stood wide to the afternoon sunshine. The heavy velvet curtains that flanked the panes were a rich burgundy. The furniture was ornate and uncomfortable-looking. Costly antiques undoubtedly. Jake liked big overstuffed furniture that was comfortable—not stylish.

The door closed behind him silently. Jake walked to the windows, pushing them open, and gazed at the formal gardens stretching out before him. Pathways wound through topiary designs. Flowers blossomed in a profusion of color, their light scents wafting on the warm afternoon air.

"Sir?"

He looked over his shoulder. The liveried footman had been replaced. His attire wasn't the uniform of the other man. He was dressed in a formal suit.

"I am Jerome, your valet. I can show you your bed chamber, if you like. I have taken the liberty of unpacking your suitcase. And I have sent out a suit suitable for tonight's dining for pressing."

Jake turned slowly to face the man.

"I don't need a valet. I don't need anyone to unpack for me and I can pick out my own clothes," he said in an even tone.

Jerome bowed slightly. "I was assigned by the king. Before his death, I served Prince Michael. I assure you I know my duty."

Jake shrugged out of his suit jacket and slung it over his shoulder, hooking it on one finger. "I never said you didn't. I just don't need anyone."

"Begging your pardon, Your Highness, but perhaps I might offer some suggestions to make your transition to living here easier. It is only a suggestion, you understand."

"I won't be living here. I'm only visiting."

Jerome's eyebrows rose in surprise. Jake almost laughed. The little man looked so comical. This was a member of the palace's elite staff?

"I am certain I was told you would be moving to Marique. That you were to be the new crowned prince. May I extend my congratulations? And, of course, my sympathy on the loss of your uncle and cousin."

"What you can offer is directions to the nearest bed. I'm beat."

"Right this way. These quarters are for visiting dignitaries. Once you have seen the family apartments and selected whichever suits you best, you can move into one of them."

Jake debated arguing the point but it wasn't worth the effort. He was here for two weeks—three weeks max. When they saw the back of him, maybe they'd realize what a visit meant.

The bedroom was as luxurious as the sitting room. A huge tester bed dominated the side wall. Ornately gilded armoires flanked each side. The lovely Aubusson carpet on the floor was worth a king's ransom. How appropriate—it belonged to a king.

Jake dropped his jacket over the back of a Windsor chair. Jerome frowned and quickly scurried forward to take it and hang it in the left armoire.

The tall windows shared the same view as the sitting room. Was that a maze in the far distance?

The valet moved to the bed and drew off the heavy brocade coverlet. He folded it neatly and laid it on a stand near the corner. He then pulled back the duvet and needlessly plumped up the pillows.

"I can manage," Jake said. "Is that a maze at the edge of the gardens?"

"Indeed it is, sir. A fine example of Paul Guilmont's work. He was an expert at convoluted confusion. It's not everyone who can find his way into the center."

"What's in the center?"

"I hear there is a charming little gazebo. Unfortunately, I'm one of those who have never made it to the center. His Majesty graciously allows the staff access to the gardens when family is not present."

Jake studied the tall shrubbery from the window. He could not discern the paths from this distance. Puzzles intrigued him. Could he find the center? If he wanted solitude, that might be the place to go. He was already beginning to feel the difference in what he was used to with liveried footmen and valets hovering.

He swung around and quickly scanned the room.

"The apartments you mentioned, are they decorated so formally?" he asked, pulling off his tie and unbuttoning his shirt. If he didn't get some sleep soon, he would fall asleep at dinner. And he had a definite opinion that would not endear him to his grandfather.

Jake paused for a moment. He was not out to endear himself to his grandfather. He was here out of a desire to right old wrongs. To make the old man pay for the heartache he'd caused his mother.

"I believe they are vacant, awaiting whatever furnishings and decorations the inhabitants might wish," Jerome said. "I shall call you in time to dress for dinner."

"Yeah, okay. But I can dress myself."

Jerome bowed slightly and left the room.

Two minutes later Jake slid between the cool cotton of the sheet and duvet. His last thought before falling asleep was wondering where Clarissa was. Had she stripped and slid into a welcoming bed wearing nothing—as he had? Too bad the two of them hadn't taken a nap together. Though sleep would have been the farthest thing from his mind if that would ever be the case.

Clarissa gave Gustine a quick kiss on her cheek.

"How was the trip?" Philippe's mother asked. She had seemed delighted to see Clarissa when she'd knocked on the door.

"Tiring. I never got used to the different time zone before we returned. I feel like it should be midnight now instead of four o'clock."

"Come and have some tea. Tell me about that man."

"I can't stay long. I really need to get to bed."

"Just for tea."

Settled in the homey sitting room, Clarissa waited for the hot beverage to be poured. There were several slices of cakes and biscuits on the tray, but she declined. She really needed to take a nap if she expected to be coherent at dinner.

But she wanted to visit Gustine first. She knew the older woman had been waiting to learn more about Jean-Antoine. How hard it was for her. Instead of her own son standing in line for the throne, he'd been succeeded by a man she'd never met.

"He's different from Philippe."

Gustine nodded. "I expected as much. Of course he has no breeding to speak of. His mother was a farmer's daughter. And he was raised in appalling circumstances."

"Through no fault of his own," Clarissa murmured in his defense. It annoyed her to realize the royal family acted as if Jake's circumstances were of his own choosing.

"Of course not. It was Prince Joseph's fault for defying his father and abandoning his responsibilities," Gustine said forthrightly.

Clarissa wanted to ask about the king's abandoning his responsibilities in not seeing to his grandson's welfare and education, but it wasn't her place to criticize the king to another member of the royal family.

"His manners are impeccable. He won't bring shame to the family."

"He has already done that," Gustine said.

"How?"

"Just by being. He'll be a constant reminder of his father's defiance. His low breeding, lack of training will be thrown into our faces all the time."

"He is very much his own man. He doesn't plan to stay."

Gustine stared at her in surprise. "Of course he'll stay. He will inherit the crown."

Clarissa shook her head. "His opinions and convictions don't match ours. He insists he is only here for a visit."

"Nonsense! I don't believe it. Once he sees what riches the king can provide, the allowance he will make, the treasures he'll be entitled to, the power that goes with the throne, he'll stay."

Clarissa remained silent, sipping her tea. It was obvious the others thought as she once had. Only somewhere along the way, she'd changed her mind. She didn't think Jake would be swayed by riches or rank.

The only thing that might make him stay was family ties, and those were too weak and frayed to hold him.

She finished her tea and placed the cup on the table.

"His Royal Highness invited me to dinner this evening. If that would prove awkward, I won't come," she said gently.

Gustine frowned. "Of course you may come. You are practically a member of the family. If Philippe had lived you two would have been married by now." She eyed Clarissa's dark suit and silvery blouse.

"You know, Clarissa, I plan to wear black forever. I'm too old and set in my ways to go looking for another husband. But you are young. Your year of mourning is over. You should not tie yourself up in memories. It would be suitable to wear bright colors again." She took a deep breath. "Even date again."

Clarissa smiled sadly. "Thank you, Gustine. When it's time, maybe." She wouldn't tell her about a yellow sweater, or riding on a motorcycle on the packed Los Angeles freeways. Or that she felt as if she were coming awake after a long sleep.

"I need to go home to rest a little while before dinner," Clarissa said, preparing to rise.

"Take your nap here. I'll send for your bags. It'll save you time driving to and from your apartment. Time enough to return there after dinner."

Clarissa quickly agreed. She was so tired, she ached. She had the dark blue evening dress she could wear. Jake had seen it already, but so what? She doubted he was the type to notice, much less comment on, women's dresses.

By the time dinner drew to a close that evening, Clarissa wondered if Jake would last the two weeks he'd allotted for his visit. She had to admire his fortitude. Since he'd first appeared in the salon where they'd met for aperitifs, he'd put up with behavior that most men would have fled.

Gustine had subtly insulted his clothing, questioned his manners in a way to suggest they were lacking, and talked around him. Even his lack of fluency in French drew her supercilious scorn.

It didn't appear to bother him. He remained cordial, polite and distant. But Clarissa knew by the slight tightening of his jaw, by the coldness in his gaze, that he was growing angrier by the moment.

The king said little during the meal, seemingly content to let his daughter-in-law run the evening.

Clarissa also spoke little. She felt awkward enough

with the king's display of surprise at her unexpected appearance. She would have thought Jake could have notified him prior to her arrival. Or Gustine.

Dessert was almost over. They were being served coffee by the well-trained footmen. Countdown until she could escape.

Jake glanced at her. Could he read minds? She sometimes thought so. The amusement in his gaze struck her. Swiftly she flicked a look at his aunt. She had been frowning all evening. His cousin Marie had been quiet as a mouse, scarcely saying three words unless addressed directly.

"Ready?" he asked, his gaze intent.

Clarissa was taken aback. Had she missed something? Were they scheduled for some activity?

"Ready for what?" Gustine asked.

Jake calmly folded his napkin and placed it to the left of his plate. He rose. From the shocked expressions on his aunt and cousin, he had to know he'd committed some faux pas.

Clarissa watched, mesmerized. No one ever left the table before the king!

"Clarissa is going to show me the gardens." He gripped the top of his chair, his manner one of casual relaxation. Only by the tightening of his fingers could she tell he wasn't as relaxed as he appeared.

"That's impossible. His Majesty hasn't given you permission to leave!" Gustine was outraged. "Besides, it's dark outside."

"I thought dinner was over. And where I come from,

no one needs permission to leave the table when they have finished eating.''

''All a part of the abominable manners you've displayed since you've arrived,'' Gustine said. ''If you had had any schooling—''

''Ah, but it's hardly my fault I wasn't trained to suit, now is it?'' Jake's voice was deadly.

She closed her mouth almost audibly. Throwing an uncertain glance at the king, she wisely kept quiet.

His Majesty rose, one of the hovering footmen dashing forward to pull his chair back.

''None of us can change the past. We can only make sure the future, as far as it is in our hands, is what we want. I expect to see you at nine in the ministers chambers. It is past time to begin your education about Marique.''

Jake said nothing, watching silently as the older man left the dining room.

''The future none of us wanted. Michael should still be crown prince. Philippe should be heir apparent. No one wanted a gold digger's brat usurping the throne,'' Gustine spat, her anger uncontainable.

''Mother,'' Marie said, realizing she'd crossed the line. ''It isn't Jean-Antoine's fault Father and Philippe were killed. He isn't pushing his way in, Grandfather summoned him. There is nothing to be done about it.''

Clarissa rose and came around. ''I'm ready,'' she said, anxious to escape the tense situation, before it became even worse.

''Rest assured, madam, I have no intention of usurping anything, as you so indelicately put it. I'm here solely for a visit. And I'm beginning to wonder why I ever came.''

Clarissa gripped his arm. "Let's go, Jake," she said softly, urgently, tugging him away from further confrontation with Gustine.

In no time they had wound their way through the corridors of the palace and descended the three wide, shallow steps that led from the back of the palace to the gardens. Soft illumination lighted the paths. Spotlights shone on the topiary designs. From the steps, a dragon appeared to rise up.

"If that's a sample of familial bliss, book me back to L.A. in the morning," Jake said once they were out of earshot of the servants that seemed everywhere. He strode off down the first path, ignoring the clipped hedge and the flowers in all their glory.

"You just got here," Clarissa said, trying to keep up. His longer stride didn't have to consider skirts and high heels.

He paused and looked at her, running his gaze from the top of her hair to her toes peeping out of the shoes she wore.

"You wore that dress in L.A. Didn't you go home?"

"I didn't have a chance. I took a quick nap, dressed and reported for dinner as ordered." She thought about snapping a salute, but in deference to his position, suppressed the urge.

"You should have told me to go jump in a lake." He slowed his pace and Clarissa walked beside him as they ambled down the pathways. She didn't think he wanted to see the gardens, only sought escape.

"With all due respect, your aunt behaved terribly."

"No kidding? I thought that was a display of the epitome of good manners. She sure harped enough on my lack of them." His voice was almost a growl.

"She's upset."

"She's a barracuda."

"Her husband and son were in line for the throne and now to see someone else—"

"I have no intention of taking their place." He stopped and looked down at her. "Read my lips. I. Do. Not. Want. To. Be. A. King."

"Gustine married Michael knowing he would become crowned prince and then king. Her second child was a male, heir to the throne. For more than thirty years, it's what she expected. She can't help her feelings."

Any more than she could, Clarissa thought wildly. Conscious of Jake's gaze, she had trouble keeping up with the conversation. She couldn't help feeling supercharged. Like she could climb mountains or conquer new worlds. The roiling emotions took the forefront, and had her wondering why they were talking about his aunt to begin with.

Colors seemed sharper. The fragrance subtly perfuming the night air seemed fresher. The nap had helped with fatigue, but being with Jake swept the last vestiges away. She felt poised on the brink of something monumentally exciting.

"I can show you the gardens," she said. "They are lovely, though much better seen during the day. I've always enjoyed wandering up and down the paths. There's always something unexpected."

She shivered, the longing for closer contact with him suddenly overwhelming. Turning abruptly, she began talking to cover the emotions that threatened to get out of hand. They'd have tonight, then she'd resume her normal duties and Jake and his grandfather would be left to figure out how to proceed from here.

"The topiary is to the left. There are some bushes over a hundred years old. The designs haven't changed for generations, though there are some newer ones in the far corner."

"The maze," Jake said. "Show me the maze."

"How did you know about that?"

"Have you ever made it into the center?"

"Once, Philippe took me."

"So he knew the key?"

"Wormed it out of the head gardener when he was little. He could charm the birds from the trees. And always wanted his own way."

"So why is my aunt appalled by me? I want my way, too. She should expect that."

"Not appalled, just reminded that her son and husband are dead and life as she always expected it to be is no more."

"Life doesn't always go as we anticipate."

"I believe for the first time I saw a glimmer of regret on your grandfather's part. I think he wishes he had made an effort to know you before now," she said diplomatically.

"Maybe, but only because of the way things turned out—not because he wants to know me. You must have noticed he never addressed a single question to me at dinner. In fact, if Gustine hadn't been on a tear, it would have been a silent meal.''

''I would have stepped in,'' Clarissa said, remembering all her hours of deportment lessons.

''Clarissa to the rescue, huh?''

''Give them some time, Jake. They are trying.''

''They are very trying!''

She suppressed another smile. He was nothing like the men she usually spent time with. Or dated. No, she hadn't dated anyone in a long time—except Philippe. And once they were engaged, even their time alone together had diminished.

Thoughtfully she remembered how much less she saw of him once she'd accepted his proposal. As if she was kept to bring out for display and put away when he had other things to do. More important things?

They drew near the opening to the maze. The shrubbery was tall, more than ten feet high, clipped tightly, so no glimmer of light came through its thickness.

She stopped at the entrance and hesitated. The pathway was illuminated, but she'd never gone in at night.

''I don't want to be wandering around in there all night. If you feel adventurous, why not come tomorrow and get one of the gardeners to show you the way.''

''No challenge in that.''

''No fun in getting lost and maybe wandering around all night. No one's working in the gardens to hear us if we call for help.''

''How long does it take to get to the center?''

''About ten minutes, I think. It was a while ago.''

"We'll mark our way, so we can get out. Let's give it a try."

She laughed. "You don't really think you'll find the center the first time, and within ten minutes?"

He shrugged. "Won't know until we try."

"You try, I'm going back inside."

"Chicken," he said softly to goad her.

"I know enough English slang to know you are impugning my honor!"

He laughed. "I love your snooty airs, Clarissa. So are you game for a challenge or not?"

"Not."

"I bet I can make it the first time."

"Never happen."

"If I do?"

"Good for you."

"Let's make it interesting."

"What does that mean?" she asked suspiciously.

He leaned closer and she was aware of being alone with him in the vast gardens of the estate. She could feel the warmth from his body envelop her. His breath caressed her cheeks.

"If I win, you give me a kiss," he said softly, gazing down into her face. The faint illumination made him look mysterious, dark as a pirate. Bold as one, too.

She felt her knees grow weak. A kiss? He wanted to kiss her?

"And if you don't?" she asked in a whisper, afraid to try a stronger tone for fear she'd give herself away.

"Ah, then I make all best efforts to charm my aunt Gustine the next time I see her."

"Deal!" She marched into the maze. She'd run to escape if she thought she wouldn't wind up in the first dead end. But his words echoed in her mind, *kiss, kiss, kiss.* She'd already wondered what it would be like. Would she ever find out?

"It still counts if you lead the way in. We reach the center, I get a kiss."

Clarissa stopped and turned to glare up at him. "I'm not leading anywhere, I merely stepped inside the maze to begin the process. Once you concede that you don't know the way to the center, you can make plans to be nice to your aunt. And I can go home and get some rest!"

He nodded, taking her hand in his. She tugged, but he wouldn't release her.

"Don't want to get separated," he murmured as he studied the path and the high leafy walls. He turned and looked behind him, then using his heel, scuffed a mark in the sandy walkway.

"What are you doing?"

"Marking our way out. I think I can figure it out, but if not, I don't want to be trapped inside a maze all night long."

She smiled smugly. "How long before you admit defeat?"

"We just started."

"Granted. I think ten minutes is too short a time, even for an intrepid explorer like yourself. But neither do I still want to be following you around at midnight. We need a time limit."

"Thirty minutes."

"You are so arrogant. You'll never find the key the first time and not in thirty minutes!"

"Two kisses says I do."

"You can bet a dozen! It's not going to happen."

Jake shrugged, and continued on. They wound up in dead ends, circled back and came across some of the markings he had made.

Clarissa was getting dizzy trying to figure out on her own if they were going anywhere, or just circling.

She was stunned when they turned the corner and came to the heart of the maze. She stopped dead and looked at the charming gazebo, brightly lit in the night darkness.

He made an elaborate display of checking his watch.

"Twenty-four minutes."

Her heart started to pound. Did he truly want to kiss her? Here? And now?

"It's pretty at night," she said, pulling on her hand. To her surprise, this time he let her go.

"I imagine it's pretty anytime." He followed the path between the two benches and stepped up into the gazebo. The gingerbread decoration made it look light and ethereal. Like a fairy's castle.

He must have found a switch, because the gazebo was suddenly flooded with soft light.

"Come and see it."

"I've been here before, remember," she grumbled as she walked slowly to the structure, feeling like a condemned prisoner walking to his fate. Only the excitement that bubbled up was unlike what a prisoner would feel.

It couldn't be anticipation for a kiss! She wouldn't permit—

He held out his hand when she stepped into the gazebo and spun her into his arms, like dance partners of old.

Slowly he waltzed them around, humming some unfamiliar tune.

Clarissa stopped worrying, stopped thinking. She gave herself up to the most romantic moment she'd ever known. His arm was strong around her, guiding her effortlessly. Their linked hands were held out, formal waltz position. Her feet scarcely skimmed the floor. She felt as light as a feather.

His dark eyes gazed into hers as he spun them around and around, never faltering in song or rhythm.

Stopping near the door, he reached out and flicked off the lights.

"I like the darkness better, don't you?" he asked softly. The ambient light from the maze paths provided enough illumination for her to see him, to see the intensity of his gaze, the slight lift to his lips.

His hand cradled her head, his fingers threaded into her hair and he tilted her face up to his.

"I've wanted to touch your hair since I first saw it. It's like silk. I wondered if it'd feel like flame, but it's cool and soft."

"Jake, we shouldn't be out here," she said, her hands coming up to rest on his arms. Her heart was pounding so rapidly she knew he must feel it. Her breath was coming in short gasps. Her mind was focusing on him and him alone.

"We had a bet."

"Did someone tell you the key?"

He shook his head slowly. "No, but I like puzzles. I must have done hundreds of maze puzzles in my time. Never got to actually go into one before tonight. Maybe I'll make one myself when I get home."

Her knees threatened to give way, the spiraling sensations that fanned out from her center were fed by his touch. Her fingertips were sensitized to the heat from his wrists. She longed to thread them in his hair, see if it felt like thick velvet, or something different.

"I figured a girl like you wouldn't want to kiss on a first date, but this is our third, so it's okay," he said whimsically.

"We haven't dated at all," she protested, not understanding why she was prolonging the suspense. Was he going to kiss her? Or was he only teasing?

"I beg to differ. Dinner at your hotel in L.A.—number one. Dinner at the beach—number two. Tonight—dinner number three. Variation on an old theme, too."

"What? Dates?" They'd not been dates. They'd been business arrangements. "I haven't dated anyone—"

"You brought me home to meet the family, too—only it was my family."

She opened her mouth to protest and he came down and captured her lips with his.

CHAPTER FIVE

CLARISSA hadn't known kissing could feel like this. His mouth moved against hers, warm and sexy, sparking excitement and a heat that threatened to consume her. She closed her eyes to better savor each explosive sensation.

When his tongue teased hers, she was lost. All thoughts of propriety and duty fled. For the first time in ages, Clarissa was living in the moment—and for herself alone.

It was the most thrilling embrace she'd ever shared. She felt as if they floated, as if time and place faded and they were in a world of two. She never wanted it to end. When he drew her closer, she didn't protest, but relished the hard wall of his chest against her softer curves, the strength of his long legs braced to hold them as his mouth continued its sweet plunder. Her own knees grew decidedly weaker.

She yearned for a closer contact, for deeper intimacy, for more and more and more. His head changed angles, deepening the kiss even further. A kaleidoscope of impressions stamped her mind—his expertise, his taste, his heat.

Suddenly it went dark.

"Dammit!" He pulled back and released her. Clarissa stumbled against the wall and leaned where she landed, gasping for breath, totally bewildered. One moment she was being kissed senseless, the next they were in stygian darkness, and she could only guess where Jake was.

She blinked, hoping she'd quickly gain night vision. Except for the sprinkling of stars in the dark sky, there was no light. The high hedges cut off any illumination coming from the palace. The grounds were totally dark.

"I didn't know they turned the lights off so early," he said.

"I didn't know they ever turned them off. I don't suppose you have a torch?" If they couldn't see, they'd never find their way out of the maze.

"What? Oh, that's a flashlight, right? Sorry, it would have spoiled the fit of my suit."

Of course he didn't have one, people as a rule didn't bring a torch to the dinner table. She looked around, widening her eyes in hopes of gaining some additional night vision.

"Since you've already pointed out the gardeners don't work at night, my guess is the lights are on a timer. So yelling would be futile—no one to hear us," Jake said. From the direction of his voice, she could tell he had moved to the opening to the gazebo.

"Someone will miss us. Gustine and Marie knew we were coming out to the gardens." Despite her best efforts, she could only clearly see the stars overhead. Everything else remained cloaked in darkness. She hadn't a clue where the path from the center even started.

"And when do you think they'll miss us, when I fail to show up at nine for the meeting my grandfather scheduled?"

"It'll be light long before nine o'clock tomorrow morning! Not that I think we have to spend the night out here. I was thinking more about when you fail to go to bed. Your valet will know something is wrong and spread the alarm."

She heard the slap of a palm against wood. "Good idea, except I told him in no uncertain terms that I didn't need his services. So scratch that idea. Were you to sleep here tonight? Will Gustine or Marie miss you before dawn?"

"Probably not. I had planned to return home." She moved gingerly away from the wall, trying to remember where she'd seen the benches. "What a mess, no one will miss either of us anytime soon."

"Oh, I don't know that it's such a mess. I'm sure we can find something to while away the night."

The suggestive tone in his voice notched up her heart rate. Clarissa let her imagination run wild thinking of ways to while away the night with Jake. Most of them included another kiss!

She found one of the benches by virtue of walking into it. Rubbing her shin, she sank down, and firmly pushed the picture of the two of them kissing the night away from her mind. She wasn't even sure, now that she was away from Jake, that she wanted a second kiss. He was not for her and she was not one for a meaningless dalliance—no matter how appealing the man.

Sexy as he was, she would want more from a relationship. And she feared Jake didn't have anything more to give her. Not that she wanted any involvement with anyone. It was too soon after Philippe's death. It might always be more than she wanted to risk.

"I think the mood's been shattered," she said dryly, hoping to circumvent discussion—or attempts at resuming where they'd left off. Her pulse still hadn't settled down. There was no denying he was potent—too much so for her.

They had more immediate problems.

"So you were in the mood?" His voice sounded sexy and tempting coming lazily from the dark.

"I paid my debt," she snapped. She refused to examine her own feelings about those kisses. And she certainly didn't plan to discuss them with Jake White. There would be no more kisses!

"Don't you have a cell phone?" she asked hopefully.

"Left it in my room. How about you?"

"In my purse, in the room where I changed." Clarissa wanted to scream in frustration. "Great, we're going to be stuck out here all night. We'll probably freeze to death and in the morning the scandal will spread like wildfire."

"Scandal?"

"You don't think people will find it outrageous that I spent the night with you when you've just arrived? I don't know about your reputation, but it'll ruin mine!"

"Spent the night is a bit extreme, don't you think. It's not like we're in some bedroom with the door locked."

"Might as well be," she muttered. There had to be some way out of the maze. Could they find the markings Jake had left in the paths? How? By crawling along the paths? She doubted that would work.

"That being the case, Aunt Gustine will have a field day. She already thinks of me as lower than whale dung."

Clarissa unexpectedly laughed. Jake's assessment of his aunt didn't seem to bother him. It occurred to her that if she had to be stranded, she was glad it was with Jake.

That sobered her instantly. She wasn't glad about anything with Jake. She should be missing Philippe, not enjoying the company of his cousin.

"Where are you?" he asked.

"If we have to spend the night out here, I don't want to stand the entire time. I found one of the benches." She rubbed her arms with her hands, chafing her skin a bit to get some warmth.

She hadn't been cool in Jake's embrace.

She shook her head, trying to dispel the thought.

She heard his footsteps and in a second, he sat beside her. Shifting to the edge of the bench, Clarissa wished it were longer. There was more than one bench in the gazebo, couldn't he have found another?

"Are you cold?" he asked as she continued to rub her arms.

"I'm fine." With him beside her, it was almost like sitting next to a furnace. She'd move farther away, but would end up on the floor. Holding herself stiffly, she thought about how much warmer she might be if she leaned against him.

She needed something else—to distract her.

"Tell me your first impressions of Marique. Is there any spark of recognition?"

"Never having been here, how could there be?"

"I don't know, some kind of family pull to this particular piece of earth. A genetic recognition of belonging."

He hesitated a moment, then shrugged. "Maybe—when I walked down one corridor where the family portraits are hung. There's a resemblance among the men that seems to be passed to each generation. I didn't get to examine them all. Are there portraits of Philippe and Michael?"

"Not in the gallery you're describing. That's for heads of state and their consorts. Your grandfather's portrait is there—when he was much younger and had just become king. And your grandmother. She was queen for twenty years before her death. Michael's official portrait would have been commissioned when he became king. There are others of him and his family, however, if you want to see them."

"An official act from my guide?"

"If you like. What else struck you today?" If she could keep him talking, there would be less time for thinking. Or kissing.

"Let's see—the king definitely does not want me here. It's all he can do to be cordial when I'm in the room. Gustine hates me. Marie is as quiet as a mouse. The palace is far more opulent than I expected. The capital city looks prosperous and vibrant. Any nightlife worth exploring?"

"There are some fine clubs and cabarets—enough to offer variety and choice," she said.

"Tomorrow you can give me a tour. Maybe even take me to visit the village where they make the soap."

"You have meetings with the king."

"Won't take long, trust me. We can get lunch out somewhere. Probably better for the digestion than eating with Aunt Gustine."

"The meetings are likely to take all day every day for a long time. There's so much history you need to learn. And our customs and traditions."

"Clarissa, you weren't listening before. I'm not going to stay here. Tomorrow the king will realize it, as well. If he kicks me out of the castle, I'll find a hotel room until I decide to leave."

She didn't respond. He had never even hinted he planned to stay, so she shouldn't be surprised by his comment. But somehow she thought he'd change his mind once he saw Marique, once he met his grandfather.

She wondered how the king really viewed his grandson. How would he take it when Jake returned to America?

How would she feel?

"Here." Jake had shrugged out of his jacket and draped it over her shoulders. She drew into its warmth. It felt heavenly.

"Won't you be cold?"

"No. Tell me more about Marique."

Clarissa tried to paint her country in glowing terms, hoping to pique his interest enough that he'd stay longer. She knew if he would get to know her country, he'd come to love it. And the people would benefit from an heir of blood. She didn't even know what to expect if he truly refused the crown. What was the order of succession if a blood-descended heir refused?

His scent surrounded her—disturbing in that it reminded her of their kiss. She had to ignore the pull of attraction and concentrate. She told him about the wonderful summers, the snowy winters, the growing tourist trade. And wondered if his scent would rub off on her. Would she still smell him if she ever reached her own home?

When she was talked out, she asked questions about his construction firm, learning about the early days when he and his partners began to specialize in luxury homes for millionaires. She was fascinated by some of the people he'd built homes for—movie stars, presidents of international conglomerates, and dot.com people who bought older houses for their location, only to raze them and build something larger and more opulent.

Without warning, the lights came on.

Clarissa blinked and looked at her watch. It was almost two o'clock in the morning.

"What in the world?"

"I don't know, but if you think they'll stay on for ten minutes, let's take a chance and run for it. Beats waiting for sunrise." Jake rose and held his hand for hers.

They hurried from gazebo and, following the marks Jake had left earlier in the paths, quickly found their way from the maze.

Jerome stood waiting at the entrance.

"Ah, sir, there you are. I was concerned when you didn't retire after others had. But discrete inquiries led me to suspect you might have been caught in the gardens after the lights were extinguished.''

''I take back all I said earlier, Jerome. You have a job as long as I am here. Can we get Miss Dubonette home without fanfare?''

''Most assuredly, sir. If you both will come this way I have taken the liberty of summoning a car for Mademoiselle Dubonette.''

They followed the man through the gardens to a service road where a limousine was waiting.

''Mademoiselle Dubonette's things are in the vehicle,'' Jerome said as the chauffeur opened the rear door.

''I'll see you tomorrow for lunch,'' Jake said as she started for the car. ''If I can get directions to your place, I'll pick you up around noon.''

She slipped out of his jacket and held it to him. ''I'm sure you can get directions. But I think you'll be tied up. You really need to give your grandfather a chance.''

''Like he gave me and my mother?''

She slid into the car without saying a word. There was nothing she could say that would ease that old hurt. Before the chauffeur could shut the door, Jake leaned inside.

''Lunch tomorrow. You can start acting like my guide. Plan to show me around the city, maybe the soap place and anything else you think's worth seeing.'' He stood and nodded to the chauffeur, turning to walk back to the palace.

Clarissa sank back against the car seat, her mind whirling. The nap that afternoon hadn't been enough to clear her head. Jet lag was playing havoc on her senses.

In addition, she now had the images and sensations from Jake's kiss to deal with.

She closed her eyes, snapping them open again when an image of Jake danced behind her closed lids. There was nothing remotely platonic about that kiss. It had been the most soul-searing, heart-throbbing, heat-producing kiss she'd ever experienced.

Frowning she tried to focus her thoughts elsewhere. Only an idiot would think of becoming involved again. She'd been engaged, lost the man she loved, and refused to expose herself to the risk of another aching loss that falling in love entailed. Especially with someone whom she knew would never stay.

She tried listing all the things she found wrong with Jake—he was arrogant, irreverent regarding her country and its king, brash, and determined to get his own way. She was afraid his way had nothing to do with the good of Marique.

But despite her best attempt, the faint hint of his scent made her heart skip a beat, had the blood zinging through her veins. She might not *like* him, but she was certainly intrigued by him.

But she needed to tread warily. She knew nothing about him beyond what she discovered in the last week. He'd told her he wasn't interested in marriage. So scratch honorable intentions. Just what were Jake's intentions?

Promptly at noon the next morning a long silver limousine slid to a quiet halt before Clarissa's town house. She'd been standing at the window for some time, lost in thought, awaiting a call canceling their outing. She knew the king would have a long list of topics to review and cover. Today's meeting would be only the first of many.

Yet when the vehicle slid to a stop, Clarissa realized she wasn't truly surprised. In the short time she'd known him, she'd already recognized Jake as a law unto himself.

She hastened to the door and opened it just as he reached it. He wore khaki slacks and a dark blue polo shirt. Aviator sunglasses hid his eyes.

"Ready?" he asked with no further greeting. From the clipped tone, she suspected his morning had not gone well.

"How did you get away?" she asked, peering behind him as if expecting to see someone trying to flag his attention.

"Do you have a car?"

"Yes."

"We'll take it rather than the limo." He turned and waved to the chauffeur. The man hesitated then bowed slightly and climbed back into the driver's seat and drove off.

Within ten minutes Clarissa found herself a passenger in her own car, Jake driving on Trans-Marique One, heading away from the capital. This route led to Chamblier and the Ambere Soap area, and through some of the most scenic portions of Marique.

When she'd protested his demand to drive, he'd countered with saying he'd get to know the area better if he

were driving. She suspected he'd have commandeered
the car no matter what excuse he came up with.

Despite her vow of the night before, she couldn't help
noticing how Jake captured her attention and held it. She
rummaged in her bag until she found dark glasses and
put them on. Hoping he was sufficiently involved with
the scenery, she studied him from the corner of her eyes.

His dark hair was thick and a bit long. His wide shoulders shrunk the size of her car. And his long legs had
the seat to its farthest position.

But it was his face that she returned to. His strong
jaw, clearly pinpointing his stubbornness to anyone who
cared to look, reminded her of the king. His high cheek-
bones, covered with tanned skin, gave his face that
sculpted masculinity. She'd seen pictures of his father,
he resembled him a lot. His lips—

He looked at her—at least she thought so, hard to tell
with the aviator glasses. "What?"

"Just wondering how you escaped your grandfather,"
she murmured.

Jake smiled sardonically. "We met at nine as requested. First thing out of his mouth was the fact he'd
hired a tutor to give me that certain polish a prince
would need."

Clarissa held her breath. She could just imagine Jake's
response to that. Frowning, she looked away. Maybe the
king should make haste slowly. She shouldn't be second-
guessing the monarch, but Jake wasn't someone to easily
take orders from someone else. Especially with the
grudge he carried.

Not like Philippe. She frowned. Philippe had nodded

and agreed to everything then went out and did whatever he pleased. At least Jake was more honest about things.

For a moment, the thought felt disloyal to Philippe. Yet it lingered.

"I told him I didn't need any polishing. That I did not plan to stay, that politics bored me and I had no intention of learning how to run a country."

"That must have gone over well," she murmured. She couldn't imagine anyone refusing a request of the king.

"He has the White temper. My mother told me my father would get angry sometimes—like a flash fire."

"LeBlanc."

"What?"

"It's the LeBlanc family. White is an American translation."

"I know that. My mother changed her name when she was denied any contact with my father's family. Petty revenge on her part, I always thought. It doesn't matter. Why does he even bother at this late date?"

"You are the heir to the throne."

Jake was silent for a long moment. "So dynasty and protocol means more than his personal views regarding his younger son and family?"

She cleared her throat. This was a minefield waiting to explode. Why was she involved? She'd done her part in getting him to Marique. She'd gone above and beyond last night in the maze. She should have firmly told him no when he asked to see her today.

Why was she agreeing—even trying to find a way to smooth things over?

"It is very important to not only the king, but the country to have you here."

"How important?" His voice was speculative.

"What do you mean?"

"Nothing, just thinking."

She studied him for a moment. "What are you thinking?"

He flashed her a grin. "Royal thoughts, what else?"

Not reassured, Clarissa grew wary.

"Tell me about the mountains I see in the distance," he asked.

Jake listened with half an ear while Clarissa talked about the scenery they were passing and the short growing season. He needed to rethink his plan to thwart the king at every move. That gave away too much. He had wanted to lead him on, have him think all is going according to his plan, then wham—show him how it felt to have his pleas come to naught. Leave him hanging like he'd left his mother hanging. But arguing with him the first morning, giving away his strategy—it wasn't like him.

He needed to keep a cool head and build a modicum of trust—then yank away the rug. When he left, the rejection would be all the more powerful for his grandfather's having thought he would get his way. And just maybe the king would have an idea how his rejection of Jake's mother had hurt—not only her but Jake himself.

Maybe once he knew how it felt he would have more respect for the blows he'd delivered to Jake and his mother all those years ago.

Not that revenge would change the past. Nor make it up to his mother. Nothing could ever mend that.

The old anger flared once again. Jake just wished he knew something that would make the old man pay for the hardships and heartache he'd caused. His mother had never asked for much. A small kindness years ago could have alleviated a lot of heartache and hardship.

Revenge sounded better all the time.

Soon Clarissa's voice penetrated his thoughts. Her voice held a trace of an accent he found beguiling. Her way of looking at him without appearing to intrigued him. Was she flirting with him?

The thought startled him. He wasn't sure he could read her correctly. Or, was it merely another assignment from the king? If he couldn't be bought with money, how about sex?

He looked at her. She turned her head quickly, peering out the window. He almost smiled. She appeared interested, but was it all a ploy? How could he find out?

Play along and see.

Their kiss last night had been unexpected. Exciting and too quickly over. He wouldn't mind exploring all facets of knowing her better. Starting with another kiss.

"Any place to eat around here?" he asked.

"There's a café in the next little town, La Rouchere, that's nice. The weather's warm enough to eat outside."

Twenty minutes later they were seated at a small table in the shade. The side street of La Rouchere held more traffic and people than Jake expected. When he commented on the fact, Clarissa nodded.

"It's market day here. There's an open-air market in

the next road. They close that street to traffic and vendors set up their stands. So that traffic and this street's normal flow are combined. Would you like to see the market when we finish eating?''

"Maybe."

"Clarissa, hello, I didn't expect to see you here.'' A tall woman dressed in black came over and gave Clarissa a cheek-kiss greeting. "Last I heard you were off to America to lure the new heir back to Marique.''

Jake leaned back in his chair, amused at the look of confusion on Clarissa's face. Was she on a mission from the king? Did she have some undercover assignment to carry out? If so, she'd have to do better than that if she wanted the role of Mata Hari. He was interested to see how far she'd carry this charade.

"I was off to America. Now I'm back. Jeannette, may I introduce His Highness, Prince Jean-Antoine.''

Damn. He hadn't anticipated that. He rose and held his hand to Jeannette. When she placed hers into his, he brought it to his mouth to brush a light kiss across the back. *"Enchanté, mademoiselle."*

"Ahhhh.'' Jeannette's hand dropped as she looked in awe at Jake, then, all aflutter, she looked at Clarissa. "I didn't expect... I mean... this is...?''

Clarissa nodded. "I'm showing him some of Marique. We just arrived home yesterday.''

"I'm so honored, Your Highness. Oh, excuse me, I didn't mean to interrupt. It was so unexpected seeing Clarissa here. And with a man. Oops. I didn't mean that. I mean.... Ah, perhaps I should go. So honored, Your Highness.'' She curtsied, then turned and walked unsteadily across the open-air café, bumping into a table before she reached the opening to the road.

Jake sat down and glared at Clarissa.

"And your reason for introducing me like that?"

"Like what? You are the prince."

"No I'm not."

She nodded emphatically. "Oh, yes. You may be reluctant to claim the title, but it's there all the same. Denying it doesn't change the facts."

"So you are trying to manipulate the outcome? By forcing the title down my throat?"

Clarissa blinked. "You didn't say anything about being incognito. We are here at your command. I'm doing the best I can, if you don't like it, get another guide."

Jake couldn't figure out her game, but he'd keep trying. "Talk like that could be considered sedition."

The waiter came over, bowing obsequiously, obviously stunned and flattered to have the royal prince at his establishment.

It took five minutes to place their order. Once the man had scurried away, Jake turned back to Clarissa.

"Another fine mess you've gotten us into, Stanley."

"What?"

He shook his head. "A quote from an old movie. My mother loved old movies. Tell me, is this something you like? All the fanfare and bowing and scraping?"

"He didn't scrape. And royalty is entitled to a certain amount of fanfare."

"Do you like it?" he persisted. Maybe that was the reason, she liked the perks that went with being with a prince.

"Not especially," she said softly.

"But?"

"There is no but. I'm more comfortable without it. But I had to get used to it with Philippe."

"Don't tell me—he loved it."

She shrugged. "I don't think he ever thought about it. He'd had it since birth."

"While I have not. Add to that, I was raised in America where we don't even have royalty. Makes me damned uncomfortable."

"There is a certain amount of protocol—"

He raised an eyebrow. "From now on, when you are showing me this country, we go incognito. No telling anyone who I am."

She bit her lip and studied him for a long moment. Jake thought he'd make his position clear, but she surprised him.

"It's only a matter of time, and I mean a short time, before your picture will be everywhere. No one in the country will miss it. You'll be recognized wherever you go."

He began to tell her to do all she could to keep his identity quiet, but reconsidered. The humiliation of his leaving would be all the greater if everyone in the country knew of his visit. Slowly Jake smiled, picturing the embarrassment when it became known he'd rejected everything including his grandfather.

Clarissa watched him. He still didn't know her role in all this. But for now, she could help him out.

"Newspapers, I presume?"

She nodded. "And the reception His Majesty mentioned last night. Those officials you don't meet between now and then, you'll meet that night. It'll officially introduce you to the nation."

"A coming of age party?"

"Sort of. You would have had it at eighteen if—"

"If my grandfather had recognized me before he was forced to do so."

The waiter came forth with their salads and beverages. Again he told Jake how his presence brought great happiness. Jake smiled and complimented the man on his locale, on the varied menus and the fact he and his companion could have privacy to eat in peace.

"Nicely done," Clarissa said when the waiter whisked the place settings from the tables immediately around them.

"My wish is his command, right?"

"Yes, Your Highness."

He began to eat. "So how far does this wish command thing go?"

"What do you mean?"

"If I say, Clarissa, kiss me like you did last night, would you?"

CHAPTER SIX

COLOR stained her cheeks. If he didn't know better, he'd suspect she was shy and embarrassed by his outspoken words. But Clarissa had been in the public light the entire time she'd been engaged. His cynicism wouldn't let him believe she was embarrassed. Yet he questioned the flush of color.

"Well?"

"No. It doesn't go that far." Her tone was stiff.

"Too bad."

But strangely, it wasn't. For some reason, Jake was pleased to know Clarissa had limits. Much as he wanted more kisses, it was good to know she was discerning and had a voice of her own.

When they finished eating, he suggested they walk to the market. Just around the corner, the street was alive with people. Colorful tarps covered individual stalls. Wandering through the wide aisles formed by the rows of stalls, Jake saw everything imaginable for sale—fresh fruits and vegetables, lamb dressed for roasting, clothing of every size, wooden artifacts, colorful scarves and tacky souvenirs to lure tourists.

Midway through the market, which stretched over four streets, he noticed a change in his reception. Vendors still smiled, but now they bowed. No longer did anyone try to pressure him to buy their products.

"Did your friend Jeannette send word?" he asked.

"Someone knew," Clarissa confirmed. She looked up. "Is it such a bad thing?"

He looked around. At least he'd gotten a feel for the place before people began treating him differently. The market would be an experience many American tourists would love.

Jake had already decided to suggest to his friend Hugh Cartier to look into building a luxury resort in Marique. This was something else to suggest to Hugh when proposing the resort. Day trip excursions to La Rouchere to provide a flavor of the country for visitors.

Mentally making a note, he turned to the nearest vendor. Time to begin to implement that plan.

By the end of the afternoon, Clarissa was exhausted. She could swear Jake spoke to every person at the market in La Rouchere. He had asked questions, complimented some of the vendors, even made suggestions for structurally improving a stall. She'd been worried for a moment he'd whip out a hammer and actually do the work.

She still wasn't sure exactly what happened, or why, but he'd charmed everyone there.

Too bad he couldn't turn some of that charm on Gustine and the king.

When they returned to her car, he'd paused near an intersection and studied the buildings, the view of the mountains through the corridor of the side street.

"It's a pretty town, don't you think?" she asked, wishing to know more, but not wishing to be rebuffed if he didn't want to respond.

"Classic European architecture. Very appealing."

He helped her into the car and then climbed into the driver's seat. "Too late to go to the soap place?"

"Yes. It would take another twenty minutes to get there. I told you it's a cottage industry, the women make it at home. By now they are preparing dinner."

"Another day, then."

"Your wish—"

"All talk and no follow-through."

"I beg your pardon?"

He brushed the back of his fingers against her cheek. "A kiss?"

She bit her lip and slowly shook her head. She knew he was teasing, but it was hard to resist. The confines of the car seemed to shrink. Her breathing came faster. His fingers were warm, soft, caressing. Why was he deliberately teasing her? He confused her totally. One minute vowing to have nothing to do with Marique, the next going out of his way to make a good impression, to meet and talk with the people in a way sure to endear himself to them beyond anything Philippe had ever done.

When he started the engine, she gazed out the window, letting the lassitude seep in. She had to stop comparing the two men. They had little in common. It wasn't fair to compare them. Philippe had been raised in royalty, raised to expect certain behavior from citizens. Jake had been raised far differently. He was harder, had more of an edge on him.

Yet his overtures of interest seemed genuine. He was a man who respected those who worked for a living.

It was an insight that surprised her. And made her

uncomfortable when she applied it to Philippe. No wonder Jake had asked a couple of times what his cousin had done. He couldn't envision anyone not working.

"You'll have to direct me from here." His comment broke into her reverie. She looked up—they were already in the outskirts of the capital city.

She told him how to get to her home, delighted the afternoon was coming to an end. It had been a strain. Yet at the same time she felt reluctant to say goodbye. Was her stint as guide ending? Or would he request her services again?

He pulled into the garage at the back of her home and stopped the car.

"You can use the phone inside to call the palace for a ride," she said as he opened the door for her. She should have thought to drop him and driven home herself.

"No need. I thought I'd get some exercise and see more of the town by walking back."

"Walking? It's several miles!"

"There'll be plenty of light." He smiled down into her face. "Besides, even if the sun sets, I suspect there are streetlights. It won't be like being in the maze at midnight."

"You don't know the way."

"Point me in the right direction. I can always stop and ask someone directions if I get turned around."

Clarissa hesitated. It seemed wrong. Yet Jake was a grown man. If he chose to walk back, so be it. She gave him brief directions and watched as he sauntered away. He still had that smooth gait she'd noticed that first day at the construction site. She could watch him for hours on end. Instead, she watched until he was out of sight.

Letting herself into her apartment, she was struck by how quiet it seemed. Empty. Like her life had been recently.

Except for today. She'd felt more alive today than in months. All because of an irritating man who was determined to deny his heritage.

Jake deliberately refrained from calling Clarissa the next two days. If he were wrong, and she was merely offering to help, two days wouldn't matter. But if, as he suspected, the king was trying to use her in some way to lure him to stay, he expected her to turn up again. Two days would be far too long a separation if she was bent on producing results.

He used the time to learn more about his family. Discreet inquiries of Jeremy elicited information about his uncle and his family. The valet was more circumspect regarding the king, but gave enough information to help Jake form an opinion of a stubborn man who had been convinced of his right when repudiating his younger son.

Keeping his thoughts to himself, Jake sat in on the briefings the king arranged for Monday morning. He learned a bit about the economics of the country, and the diverse opinions of the king's ministers regarding their future direction. When they almost slid into a shouting match, he became more alert. When tempers were heated was a time when hidden truths were revealed.

He drew the line at the king's attempts to polish his manners. His mother had done her job, he didn't need coaching from someone the king appointed. Though he did listen to Jeremy when he explained the protocols for formal receptions. Sounded like a lot of ritual that meant nothing in the twenty-first century. Would he have felt differently about everything if he'd been raised in Marique?

On the third morning since he'd seen Clarissa, Jake ate his breakfast on the balcony of his suite. He found meals tedious with Aunt Gustine, so only ate dinners with the family when required. The rest of the time, they left him alone, which suited him perfectly.

Jeremy appeared on the balcony. "Sir, your cousin Marie is here, wishing to speak with you."

"Send her out. And get some coffee for her."

Marie stopped in the doorway, looking around with curious eyes. She smiled shyly at Jake and stepped onto the balcony.

"Sorry to bother you at breakfast."

"You're not bothering me. Come and sit down."

She walked over and perched on the edge of a chair, looking as if she would flee at the slightest provocation.

Jeremy appeared a moment later and carrying a tray with a silver coffeepot and china cup and saucer. He placed them on the table, and quickly and efficiently placed the cup before Marie, pouring the hot beverage.

Jake offered her a croissant from the tray piled high, but she declined.

"It's nice today," she said, taking a sip of coffee.

"The weather has been beautiful since I got here. I bet it's quite different in the winter."

She nodded.

The silence stretched out. Jake finished his own coffee and leaned back in his chair, studying his cousin. He'd been in residence almost a week and didn't know a thing about her. She rarely spoke at dinner, and he had not seen her at any other time.

"Is there something I can do for you?" he asked as the silence continued.

She shook her head nervously. "No. Should I go? I really came to visit. Only I can't think how to start a conversation without sounding terribly nosy."

"So be nosy. If you ask a question I don't want to answer, I'll tell you."

"Oh. Very well. Tell me something about life in America. I've always wanted to visit that country."

"So go."

"Oh, I couldn't."

"Why not? I understand your brother traveled extensively."

She nodded, her dark hair brushing against her shoulders. "He did, but he was a man. It wouldn't be proper for me to travel without an entire entourage, and that's not the way I want to see America."

"How do you want to see it?"

She sighed. "Just go. Do things a normal person does. Maybe even drive a car all by myself. Eat when I wanted, where I wanted. Try fast-food hamburgers and pizza and other American food. See Disneyland."

Marie surprised him. As their conversation continued,

he learned more about the restrictive life she'd led—such a contrast to the wild exploits of her brother. He told her about L.A., and she soaked up every word. Some of her comments had him chuckling—seeing things differently from her eyes.

It was sometime later when Jeremy again appeared at the door to the balcony.

"Sir, the king has summoned you for another meeting."

"I'll be right there."

"Oh, I've been too long." Marie jumped up.

Jake rose. "Come again tomorrow. We can have breakfast together. I'll tell you more about Southern California."

"That would be wonderful. I wouldn't be intruding?"

"No." He hadn't had breakfast with anyone in a long time. Maybe he'd enjoy the novelty. He found his younger cousin appealing. And as far as he could tell, she had no ulterior motives in talking with him. No animosity to spew forth, no duty-before-all-else attitude. Just a lonely young woman wanting to get to know her cousin.

She had given him things to think about. At least one member of his family liked him. And he liked her.

When he was escorted to the conference room, Jake did some serious thinking. He was becoming familiar with the palace. Next time he knew he could find his way without a guide.

Or wasn't he trusted to wander around the place by himself?

Stepping into the conference room, he paused a moment, surprised to see only Clarissa Dubonette seated beside the king at the long, polished mahogany table.

So, the game continued. He schooled his features and nodded in greeting. What was the next step between the king, Clarissa and himself?

She smiled uncertainly, looking guilty about something.

"Come in, come in." The king was in his usual testy mood.

Jake walked up to the table, sitting opposite Clarissa. Interesting, he thought, his gaze flicking between the king and her. He hadn't called her, yet here she was again. It went beyond coincidence. She and the king were definitely up to something.

"Good morning, Your Highness," she said.

He glanced at the king. No doubt her formality was directly due to his presence.

"I've asked Clarissa to join us this morning. You and your aunt don't seem to be getting along as well as I had hoped."

Jake had difficulty keeping his expression neutral. His grandfather had seriously expected him and his aunt to get along? Amusement filled him. The man lived in a fantasy world, and not just because of the palace.

The king glared at him. "It's your fault, of course."

"Of course," Jake murmured.

When he said nothing further, the king looked at Clarissa. "I've asked Clarissa to assist you in whatever manner you need to furnish your apartment. She and Philippe were planning to marry, you know. They had begun to furnish quarters in the palace. She's practically

a member of the family. She'll be able to help with furniture, decorators, whatever.'' He waved his hand about
as if encompassing all involved in furnishing a home.

"I've put you in the west wing. It'll give you the
privacy you seem to want.''

"In other words, it's as far from the others as I can
get,'' Jake said.

The king looked at the high gloss on the conference
room table.

"They're the quarters Joseph had before he left for
America,'' he said softly.

Jake was surprised. His father's quarters? He wouldn't
have thought the king had that much sentimentality in
him.

He glanced at Clarissa. Her eyes were fixed on him,
almost flashing in heat. If he were a betting man, he'd
wager she was majorly angry. At him? At the king? At
the assignment?

"No rush. The quarters I have are fine,'' Jake said.
He wasn't going to be here long enough to furnish an
apartment, much less live in it. His inherent dislike of
waste rose. Why needlessly spend the money or energy?

"Those are guest quarters. As long as you are there,
it's as if you are visiting.''

"I am visiting,'' Jake said easily.

"Nonsense. This is your home. You need to get settled. There will be a lot to do in the next few months.''
The king rose and looked at Clarissa. "I'm depending
on you, Clarissa.''

Once the king left, Jake stood up. He'd interrupted his

conversation with Marie for this? He headed for the door.

"Jake, wait!" Clarissa scrambled up from her chair and came around the end of the table toward him.

"I'm not staying. You know that. I know that. And in a few more days, the king will know that. There is nothing to be done about any apartments."

"Would you have me disobey a directive?"

"Do you know where these apartments are?"

"Yes."

"Then let's go. I'd like to see where my father once lived."

She opened the door and led the way down the hall. It took several turns and a flight of stairs before she opened one of a double set of carved doors. There was a small entryway, opening into a large, empty room. The ceilings were twelve feet high, an ornate chandelier was draped in dust covers, cobwebs adorning it. Dark drapes were drawn over windows, heavy with dust. The carpet underfoot, once vibrant and rich with color, now looked faded and tired in the dim light.

Jake stood in the entryway and surveyed the room. No furniture. A fireplace against an inside wall, with gilt trim on the mantel. An air of neglect hung over everything.

"It's a complete, self-contained apartment," Clarissa said. She crossed to the left, and disappeared through another door. After a moment, Jake followed her.

He glanced around, trying to imagine what kind of life his father had here. Did he bring his dates to the apartment? Did princes date? Or were their relationships dictated by dynastic concerns?

Stepping into the next room, he noted it resembled the first with its air of neglect. Probably it had been used as a dining room. He walked to the windows and pushed aside the heavy velvet curtains. Dust showered down on him. The windows overlooked the gardens. He mentally calculated where he was in relation to the rest of the palace.

"There's a kitchen through here, and another entry so the cook and maids don't have to use the front door."

"You sound like a real estate agent pointing out all the benefits of a place to a reluctant buyer."

"Do you want to see the kitchen?" A touch of asperity colored her tone.

He shook his head. "Bedrooms?"

"Three." She headed back to the first room, and on through an archway on the far side. He heard doors opening. Sliding his hands into the pockets of his slacks, he slowly walked back in that direction.

For the first time since he had been a kid, he wondered about his father. His mother had adored him, and would never say a bad word about him. Yet from the few stories she told, Jake had a mental picture of a selfish, self-centered, spoiled playboy who thought he could have anything he wanted in the world and damn the consequences.

That Joseph had loved his mother, Jake never had any doubts. But a more responsible man would have made sure she and their child would be provided for should anything happen to him.

Not that most men expected to die so young, but Joe LeBlanc had dared death with his myriad of exploits. Flying, racing, deep-sea diving and other activities weren't in the same risk category as going to a routine desk job every day.

"I think this is the one your father used," Clarissa said, standing beside an open door. "He left home when he was twenty-two, never to return. Your aunt Gustine once said it took his mother years before she could bear to come into the apartment. It was closed up after her death."

Jake stood in the doorway. There was nothing in this room, either. All trace of his father had been removed. His grandfather's doing?

He spun around and headed for the door. He'd seen more than enough.

He waited for Clarissa at the front door. "You'll have to come up with some reason to stall the king for a couple of weeks. Once I'm gone, the assignment will be rescinded."

"What am I supposed to do in the meantime?"

He paused and looked at her. "Find out all you can about the apartment. Talk to Gustine or the king. Find out what happened to the things that belonged to my father."

"And then?"

"And then let me know." He nodded once and left, heading straight for his rooms.

He was scheduled for another meeting with the minister of education. His days at home were similar, more meetings than actual site work. Despite his intentions, he was interested in learning more about the country. In one aspect, it was similar to running a large business. As long as the right manager was matched with the right job, it would run smoothly.

But today, instead of paying strict attention to the outline of policies and procedures, Jake's mind wandered. To Clarissa. He had half expected to see her again. And was amused by the king's blatant machinations. It didn't take much to see he was scrambling for a reason to throw them together. Outfitting an apartment? Wasn't that a bit obvious?

"Any questions, Your Highness?"

He came back to the meeting at hand. "You did a masterful presentation. If I might have a few days to study the material you prepared, I'd be in a better position to inquire after any points that weren't already made clear."

The minister beamed, exchanging glances with the others. Jake wondered if the man had any idea he hadn't heard a word he'd said.

When the proper formalities had been observed, Jake gathered the folder and bid the others farewell. He walked back to his quarters, feeling restrained and restless. What he'd really like to do was find a motorcycle and head for the hills—literally. He'd like to see more of the countryside and explore the tiny kingdom.

He opened the door to his rooms and stopped when he saw Clarissa sitting on the sofa.

"Finished the briefing already?" she asked, jumping to her feet.

He lifted the folder. "What I didn't get at the meeting,

I'm sure is covered in here.'' He tossed it on the side table and walked over to her.

''What are you doing here?''

''I have that information you requested.''

''What information?''

''About your father's things. And his life here before going to America.'' She gestured to a thick photo album lying on the coffee table. ''I talked to Gustine as you suggested. She gave me a lot of details about your father and threw in an album with family pictures.''

Jake stared at her for a moment, then glanced at the album. He felt as Pandora might have felt—curiosity burning. Dare he open a page on the past?

CHAPTER SEVEN

CLARISSA stood quietly, wondering if she should leave him with the album, or first tell him the things Gustine had revealed.

She studied him while he paced. He was wearing a suit which fit perfectly. He looked like the successful businessman he was. How could the king and his other relatives not see it? How could they still think he was a mere laborer with no education or sophistication?

The king had told her to use her expertise to make sure Jake's apartment was furnished tastefully and according to his rank. She felt uncomfortable knowing the truth when his grandfather didn't. But she had given her word and wouldn't break it without strong provocation.

Jake paused and looked at her, his own expression assessing. "Did you eat lunch yet?"

Clarissa shook her head slowly, her heart rate increasing with that look. His dark eyes seemed to see right down through her. His expression was designed to give nothing away, yet penetrate her own defenses and leave her feeling vulnerable.

How had he perfected it? She tried, but he kept reading her mind. She hoped he couldn't do so today. Or he'd know how torn she felt.

He made her angry and upset with his talk and plans of revenge. And by the fact he didn't seem to be even

118

trying to get along with his grandfather or aunt. It wouldn't hurt to meet them halfway. Though maybe finding halfway would be hard—they didn't appear to be making any overtures, either.

On the other hand, his behavior perplexed her. He'd wandered through the open-air market last Saturday with a genuine interest in the people and their tasks. He asked intelligent questions. He'd walked home from her house to see more of the capital city. And she'd bet he talked to people he encountered and made a favorable impression on anyone he met.

He was going through the motions with his grandfather's briefings. Yet he still planned to leave in little over a week's time.

He wanted nothing to do with the king, yet he wanted to know about his father.

"Come with me, then," he said.

"Where?" It would be better if she spent as little time with him as she could. How would she face the king if he asked her later if she'd known of Jake's plans? How could she say she did and had done nothing to warn him? How had her loyalties changed to Jake from her king?

"I don't know. First I have to see if I can get wheels." Jake went to one of the tapestry bellpulls and yanked.

Instantly she remembered his wheels in California— a shiny black motorcycle. She didn't think the palace ran to motorcycles.

He grinned at her. "There are some aspects about this that come straight from King Arthur and the Round Table. Are there any knights in the country?"

She shook her head. "No, but there are other members

of the aristocracy. We've never had a fighting army, and knights started out as loyal men-at-arms for kings.''

Jeremy appeared in the door. ''May I assist?''

''Do you lurk in the hallway in case I ring?'' Jake asked whimsically.

''I hope I know my duty, sir. It is not to keep you waiting.''

Jake winked at Clarissa. Speaking to Jeremy, he said, ''I need a vehicle. I want to go to lunch and then see some more of Marique. Miss Dubonette has graciously consented to show me around.''

''I can call for a limousine.''

''No. We want our own car. Something that will take the curves and let us see the scenery.''

''The garage houses a number of vehicles,'' Jeremy said formally. ''There is a nice Mercedes convertible that would enable you to see our spectacular scenery to best advantage.''

Clarissa felt her heart catch. Was it the car that had been Philippe's? If she'd been asked, she would have said it had been sold after his death. It felt odd to think it was still here and he was gone.

''No motorcycle?'' Jake asked.

Jeremy merely shook his head. No trace of surprise showed at the question.

''Then the convertible it is. Have it brought 'round, we'll leave in five minutes.''

''Very good, sir.'' Jeremy bowed slightly and exited as silently as he'd come.

''Today we'll go all the way to your village to see the

soap production. And while we drive, you can fill me in on what my aunt told you.''

In five minutes they were settled in the car. When she'd first seen it, she thought of Philippe, but by the time Jake had started out into traffic, all thoughts of her former fiancé had fled. She couldn't ignore the man beside her.

She'd known his cousin most of her adult life. But somehow Philippe had faded into a shadowy figure. Jake was real, almost larger than life.

Was it because he was still so much a stranger? Or was it that his energy was amazing? Or the constant tug of attraction that she felt around him had her more confused than ever?

She didn't want to fall for another man. Especially one who had been clear from day one he had no intention of staying in Marique. They had nothing in common. Her family lived here. Her roots were in Marique. His were in America.

She felt loyal to the king and crown, he actively disliked both.

If she ever felt in the position to risk her heart again, she'd want someone who shared her heritage and background. Someone easy to love and to be loved by. Not the cauldron that was Jake White.

But sometimes the heart didn't listen to the head.

She had better do all she could to maintain her distance! Already when they were apart, she spent a lot of time dwelling on the times they spent together. And remembering their kiss in the maze. Wondering what it would be like to convince him to stay. To see if this attraction could develop into more.

Becoming involved in family revelations wasn't the way to keep a distance, she thought wryly. Jake should have talked to Gustine directly, or to his grandfather. She didn't relish her role.

"The king is going ahead with the reception next Saturday. I assume you'll be my escort," Jake said as they headed out of town. She didn't have to give any directions today. Had he been driving already? Or just studied some maps before venturing out?

"I doubt you'll be expected to have an escort. Such things give rise to speculation."

"Such as?"

"Is the woman in question in the running to be the future princess of the country."

"Dynastic maneuvering. So far you pop up all the time. I didn't see anything different about next Saturday."

"I'm sure you're entitled to invite anyone you wish."

"Like I know a lot of women in Marique. Let's see, there's Aunt Gustine, whom I wouldn't invite to cross the street with. Marie, who is turning out to be an interesting young woman, but is my cousin. And you— odds on favorite."

"I'm sure an escort is not necessary," she said stiffly. She wasn't sure she wanted to attend at all. And to go with Prince Jean-Antoine as he was introduced to the country could give rise to speculations she didn't want to even imagine. Would everyone else think as Jake had upon meeting her that she'd thrown her cap after the next heir apparent in order to insure a shot at becoming queen?

"I'm not sure you or I have a choice if we don't want to rock that boat. So what did my aunt have to say?"

She pushed aside the question of the reception and began to tell him some of the stories Gustine had told her. Understanding Gustine's biased view, Clarissa tried to balance the tales with what she'd heard growing up and some of the comments Philippe had made.

It was after two o'clock by the time Jake parked the car on a side street in Ambere. Clarissa suggested they try a lovely restaurant near the edge of town. Built on a cliff, the floor-to-ceiling windows on the outside wall provided a spectacular view. And as late as they were for lunch, service should be quick.

The maître d' greeted them, bowing and speaking rapidly in French.

Jake looked at Clarissa.

She quickly told the man Jake spoke English. Immediately he switched to that language.

"You do our establishment much honor, Your Highness. If you will come this way, I will show you the best table we have."

Jake let Clarissa precede him, murmuring softly for her alone, "Did you tell him?"

She shook her head.

Once the menus had been presented with a flourish and the maître d' had bowed out, Jake looked at Clarissa.

She couldn't help the smile. "Your picture has been in the newspaper for three days now, complete with story about how the king has been reunited with his long-lost grandson. I bet there isn't a man or woman in the entire country who wouldn't recognize you.''

''Not reading French, I have not seen a paper. Where did the picture come from?''

''I have no idea where it came from, but it's a formal portrait. You look very serious in it.'' And sexy as could be, but she didn't think she needed to share that opinion. She wondered what the other women in the country thought when they saw it.

''And the purpose of splashing my face across the paper?''

''To reassure the people of Marique the continuation of monarchy is assured,'' she answered quietly, a prick striking her heart.

She wished it were so, but feared the fallout when Jake departed.

He looked at his menu.

''You don't seem upset to learn about the articles,'' she said, wanting some reaction.

Shrugging, he glanced at her. ''Should I be?''

''Are you still leaving?''

He nodded.

Clarissa dropped her gaze to her menu, but didn't see the words blurring before her eyes. She was beginning to understand the form of revenge Jake had chosen. He was leading the king on, making him think he was staying. The blow would be devastating when he left. Especially after all the articles and the formal reception.

''Don't do this, Jake. We don't deserve it.''

He met her gaze. ''And I deserved the treatment from my father's family when I was a child?''

"Let the past rest. Nothing can change it. But amends can be made."

"My mother is dead, how do you make amends to her? She did nothing wrong. Except to love a man who died young. His family ignored her, labeling her a gold digger. They never even met her or gave her a chance."

"I know it's impossible to make it up to your mother. But your grandfather is the only member of your family you have left, beside Marie. Get to know him. Forgive the past mistakes. Let the future hold something different for you and for him."

"Is this the king's emissary speaking?"

She hesitated. There was more involved than representing the king. But she wouldn't give Jake that kind of ammunition. She dare not risk his suspecting.

The waiter arrived, saving her from responding.

Quickly selecting her choice for entrée, she placed the photo album on the table. She'd already told him as much about his father as Gustine had told her. Flipping open the pages, she stopped at the one of Joseph shortly before his last trip to America. She pushed it over to him, tapping the photograph with a fingertip.

"That's your father. You two look alike. I'm sure your grandfather sees that every time he looks at you."

Jake studied the photo for a moment. "My mother had a couple of photos of him on her bedside table. Just snapshots. But they were there until the day she died."

"She must have loved him very much," Clarissa said gently.

"So she said every time I'd ask her why she didn't go out on dates. She said she had loved only one man."

He looked pensive. "She never found anyone else she liked enough to date more than once."

"The king and your aunt misjudged your mother."

"Purely on preconceived ideas, too."

"Don't do the same."

He studied her for a long moment. "Stay out of it Clarissa. I don't want you to get hurt."

She nodded, raising her chin slightly. He was right, it was none of her business.

He flipped through the album, looking at the photographs, pausing now and then to study one closely.

"That's your uncle, Michael. He and Joseph were quite different, for all accounts. I never met your father, of course, but I knew Prince Michael fairly well—or at least as well as any woman knows her future father-in-law. They were apparently nothing alike. He was in his forties when I first met him. But even so, the stories Philippe used to tell never indicated Michael was the hell-raiser your father was."

"Maybe he always knew his duty and acted accordingly."

"I suspect so. Or maybe the hell-raising gene just skips around. Philippe had it, I'd say. Are you a hell-raiser?"

Jake shook his head. "Not me, I've always followed the straight and narrow." The gleam in his eye belied the words.

Clarissa didn't believe him for a moment. But he didn't display that restlessness that Philippe had. Or that she suspected his father had.

"It would be interesting to see if it skips around and

how any kids I could have had turn out," Jake said, turning the page and studying another set of photographs.

She remembered their discussion at the beach. Neither planned to marry or to have children. Had something changed his mind?

She felt a pang that she wouldn't see his children— most likely a dark-haired boy who loved to build things. Or a little girl with glossy dark curls, who would wrap her father around her little finger.

She wished she could know what kind of father he'd make—though she suspected he'd be a great one. He'd lavish all the love he'd missed on his children and make sure they were provided for in case something happened to him. If he returned to America as he said, she'd likely never see him again. Never know if he married, or had those children.

"You'll have to write to me and let me know about your children when they are grown and set on their paths in life," she said. It would be something, to hear from him in the future. To keep some kind of tie with him.

He nodded, his dark eyes holding hers. "If I ever have any kids, it's a deal. But I don't plan on it."

Their meal was quickly served—succulent lamb in a savory sauce. Their talk centered around the photos in the album and as much of his family history as Clarissa knew.

"Tell me about your family," Jake said after listening to an amusing story about Marie and Clarissa in Paris several years earlier. "You don't talk about them a lot."

"Only because I'm trying to bring you up to speed

on yours. I have two sisters, both are married. I have three nieces and a new baby nephew.'' For the rest of the meal, Clarissa regaled him with stories of her own family.

Jake listened attentively. He was learning a lot more about the woman than she probably guessed. The way her face lighted up when she spoke of her nephew and nieces, showed how much she loved them, and children in general. The warmth in her voice when she talked about her parents let him know she valued them and their contributions in her life. She'd had a strict upbringing but didn't chafe against it like Marie.

He was interested in hearing how she'd become involved in the soap business, and her hopes and dreams for expansion. Not for herself, but to give the women who worked in it a chance to do more for their families.

By the time they walked across the village to meet some of the soap producers, Jake had a much better understanding of his companion. And was beginning to believe she had been chosen for her tasks simply because the king trusted her. Perhaps there was no ulterior motive in her involvement, after all. Suspicions died hard, but he was willing to give her the benefit of the doubt.

He watched her lips as she talked, and longed to feel them again under his. Heard her laughter and longed to hear it in the night, when they were both wrapped up in each other. Her voice was low and melodic. How sexy would it sound in the dark of midnight?

As they walked, her arm brushed against his and it was all he could do not to reach out and thread his fingers through hers, to feel that soft skin, to have her palm against his.

Wouldn't that shock her and the locals? For a moment he was tempted. But he knew he wasn't staying. It wouldn't be fair to tempt gossip that could hurt her when he was gone.

Despite her concerns, he was fully aware of his actions, and the ramifications his defection would cause. Deliberately he continued with his plan. His grandfather would suffer because of his treatment to Jake's mother, but that was only right—he had been the one to cause the trouble when his son had died.

While it served his grandfather right, Clarissa had done nothing to deserve such treatment. Despite her assignment as emissary of the king, she'd been kind to him—even when she thought he was a common laborer.

He let Clarissa take the lead in the tour. She proudly explained the different stages and steps from beginning to finished product. The women respected her and were obviously flustered to have the prince of their country visit.

He found he was more interested in the small industry than he'd expected. On their way back to the car, he asked her how it could expand.

"When we save enough money, we'll be able to build a small processing center. Right now, as you saw, everything is done by hand in the individual homes. If we had a small plant, we could produce more and probably at a lower cost. We wouldn't want to get so large we couldn't maintain quality control. Anyway that's our dream. To that end we save ten percent of gross receipts.''

"And your marketing?''

She explained what she was doing, how they targeted quality boutiques throughout Europe, especially in resort towns where tourists were more likely to spend freely.

They reached the car. He opened her door, pausing a moment.

"I have some venture capital friends who might be interested in investing in a company with a lot of potential. Shall I have them contact you?''

Clarissa blinked. Jake loved the expression. Once again he was struck at how open she was. No one ever needed to worry about where they stood with Clarissa. Her expression would instantly let them know—if they caught it before she smoothed it out and took on her professional persona.

He knew she was upset about his plans to leave. That she loved her country, and her family. And she respected and admired the women who worked from home making soap. What more could he learn in the days he had left?

"That would be terrific. Would they invest only? They wouldn't want an ownership part of the business, would they?''

"You can discuss terms with them. I'll have a couple call you. You decide which you like and if you want to deal with them or not.''

When he climbed behind the wheel, she turned slightly to face him.

"Why would you help when you're planning to leave?''

He stared out the windshield for a long moment before speaking. "My feelings for my grandfather are personal. But if I can help in other areas, why not? It's no more than my cousin would have done, surely."

She was silent so long, he looked over at her.

"What?"

"Actually, Philippe thought this was silly. Making soap. He used it at the palace, but said if we didn't make any, there were lots of brands out there and he'd still be clean."

"Was this before or after you two became involved?"

"I think he had the feelings all along. But he said that to me after I started doing the marketing."

"So tell me again about this paragon of a cousin. What did he do to help the country?" he asked as he started the car and backed from the parking place.

"He was an ambassador of goodwill, I told you that. His father was next in line for the throne. Philippe would have done more when he was crowned prince."

"Or not. If he was as restless and reckless as my father, it's no wonder he killed himself."

"It was an accident!"

"So what did you see in him? Sounds like he was gone more than he was here. And when home, didn't do much for your beloved country. I can't see the two of you getting married, from what I've learned about you and heard about him. What was the appeal?"

Clarissa became silent. Jake wondered if she'd ever tell him. He concentrated on his driving, enjoying the air whipping by, and the spectacular view along the curvy mountain road. He wanted to venture further west to see how that part of the country looked. But not today.

He'd spoken to Hugh Cartier and told him about opportunities in an unspoiled country for an elegant resort. Hugh was flying in at the end of the week to check it out. The head of the expensive Cartier Resorts, Hugh was always looking for opportunities for expansion.

He'd almost forgotten the question when Clarissa spoke again. "Philippe was always so much fun. He made me feel extra special. He was glamorous and carefree and dashing and when he turned his attention to me, I felt glamorous, as well. He didn't do much for our country except represent it at foreign events. But don't judge him, Jake. He didn't grow up like you did. He didn't have the hardships that you overcame. Didn't have time to develop a work ethic. Thinking about it, he was spoiled, but that wasn't his fault."

"I never said a word."

"I could tell you don't think very highly about him," she muttered.

He flicked her a glance.

"Glamour, huh, like what?"

"I don't know, coming unexpectedly to take me out to dinner and dancing. Or a drive." She rubbed the leather seat absently. "This was his car, you know."

Jake's hands tightened on the wheel. "I'm sorry Clarissa, I didn't know or I wouldn't have taken it."

"It doesn't matter. It only holds good memories. We'd drive along the highway, going fast, of course. Philippe did like speed. Maybe he wouldn't have been satisfied staying here any more than you are."

"Or maybe he was sowing wild oats and would have settled down when the time came." Jake didn't want to alter her memories. But he wondered again why she had loved his cousin so much.

"Do you think, given time, your father might have?" she asked unexpectedly.

"I have no idea. I never knew him. But from what my mother said, he was spoiled rotten and thought he was immune to the laws of men and physics. I expect even if he had not met her, he would have tumbled into trouble and ended up dead long before he should have."

"But maybe he would have come back home and made things right with his father first."

"Maybe. But if he was as stubborn as his father, I doubt it."

Jake remembered the way to Clarissa's apartment and drove straight there when they returned to the capital city.

When he stopped at the curb, she looked at him uncertainly. "Do you want to come in?"

"Not today, but I'll take a rain check." He wanted to see her home, to be alone with her away from the palace with no chance of Jeremy or another servant softly entering unexpectedly. But not today.

Jake still wasn't sure what to think about Clarissa. Was she friend or spy? He wanted to kiss her and hold her and have some of that enthusiasm she displayed that afternoon focused on him.

They'd both said they weren't looking for commitment. He'd make sure he did nothing that could rebound on her once he left. And tomorrow he'd show her an American could be just as exciting as a Marique prince.

Damn, he *was* a Marique Prince. How could he have forgotten—even for a moment?

And the reason? To show her he could offer her as much as his cousin? No, there was more than that. He wanted Clarissa. Maybe his gesture would make sure they had a chance to be together.

He walked her to the door.

"I'll call you later," he said.

She inclined her head. "As you wish."

He smiled at that. "Hold that thought."

"I left the album in the car. Gustine said you could keep it as long as you wanted."

"Think she's mellowing?"

"I doubt it, I suspect she wants to show you all you missed." Clarissa snapped her mouth shut, her expression stricken. "Sorry. You don't need to be reminded of that."

"No. But talking about it can't hurt. Don't be afraid to say whatever you want around me, Clarissa."

"Then, I hope you can give some thought to furnishing that apartment. Even if you return to America next week, maybe you could come back from time to time."

Jake shook his head. "To what end? Still hoping I'll change my mind."

"Do you blame me?"

"No, I might be tempted if I was in your place. Thanks for the tour. I'll have Jason and Harvey give you a call. You decide which might offer the better deal, but don't be hasty in that decision."

He brushed his lips against hers, tapped her chin with his finger and left.

Clarissa stood staring after him, flustered at the way he kissed her so casually—as if he had the right. Then she began to wonder what she would have done if he'd wanted more than a casual kiss.

An hour later when the phone rang, she hurried to answer it, sure it was Jake.

"Pack a bag and be ready to leave for Paris in the morning. I'll pick you up about ten," he said.

"Paris?"

"Need to see what I want to furnish the apartment with, wouldn't you say?"

"Do you?" Was he thinking of coming back? Her heart leaped with gladness.

"No, but it sounded good. Marie is going with us."

"Oh?" The disappointment seemed out of proportion.

"It ticked off Aunt Gustine, so I figured it was in a good cause. And the girl needs to get out more. She wants to visit America, you know. But her mother thinks she'll stay like my father did, so won't let her go. I guess she didn't worry about her son doing so. Anyway, ten tomorrow. Bring something for dinner and dancing." He hung up before Clarissa could think of a response.

Slowly she placed the receiver back on the phone. What was Jake up to? She laughed softly. She'd bet anything it was an attempt to outdo his cousin.

Not that he needed to do anything. Just his being outdid his cousin. But she didn't think she'd tell him just yet. A couple of days in Paris sounded like it could be fun. Especially with a stranger who proved perplexing, demanding and totally irresistible.

CHAPTER EIGHT

PROMPTLY at ten the next morning a chauffeur knocked on Clarissa's door. She showed him her bags and followed to the car. When he opened the door, she joined Jake and Marie in the back.

"Hi, Clarissa. Isn't this great!" The younger girl was bubbling with excitement. "We're going to stay at the George Cinq. And I get to do whatever I want! No chaperone, no guardian!"

Clarissa smiled at Marie's excitement. She greeted them both, but her attention was immediately fixed on Jake. He looked terrific today. And his lazy perusal of her set her nerve endings fluttering. She tried to maintain her composure, but with her heart pounding and every cell attuned to the man, it was difficult.

"So this is a shopping expedition?" she asked as she settled in the comfortable cushions.

"No, that's our cover," Marie said. "Perfect, don't you think?"

"Our cover? Are we being clandestine?"

"Definitely. Marie is spreading her wings. And we are not to interfere. You and I have other plans," Jake said.

Clarissa looked at Marie and back at Jake. "What plans?"

"You'll see."

The royal jet was waiting and took off with minimum fanfare, soon landing in Paris where another limousine awaited. Once they checked into the George Cinq, Marie gave Jake a hug. "Thanks so much, cousin. I'll meet you back here promptly at four tomorrow!"

"Don't get in trouble," he warned.

She laughed and almost danced away. "I'm going to have a great time. No trouble allowed."

Clarissa watched her leave the lobby. "Where is she going?"

"Wherever she wants," he said, pocketing their keys and heading toward the elevators. "I thought we could unpack and then wander along the Left Bank. You can show me what you like about Paris."

"Have you been here before?"

"Once or twice."

"What do you like?"

"The nightlife."

Clarissa wondered who he'd shared nightlife with before. Not that it mattered, she was curious. Merely curious.

"And Marie?"

"This is a test. If she does all right alone here in Paris, where she's been before, then we're trying the U.S."

"What does that mean?"

They stepped into a vacant lift and were swiftly carried up to their floor.

"Marie wants to visit America, but without an entire entourage. So if she's comfortable wandering around by herself here, she'll try L.A. Visiting me, of course."

"Your aunt will have a fit!"

Jake smiled.

He stopped by a door and opened it, reaching for her hand and dropping the key into it. "This is your room. Mine is farther down the hall. Marie has the one across from you. How long to unpack? Can you be ready in, say, thirty minutes?"

"Yes." It had been a short flight. She didn't need to do anything but hang up her dresses and check her makeup. Then, she and Jake would be spending the rest of the day and evening together—alone in the City of Lights.

She narrowed her eyes suspiciously. "Why are we really here?"

He leaned negligently against the doorjamb and folded his arms across his chest. "To show you Philippe wasn't the only one capable of sweeping you off your feet. Today and tonight, we'll do whatever you want. Wander where our fancy takes us. Sip champagne at the Savoy, and dance the night away."

"And what do you get out of it?" she asked. She refused to examine exactly how pleased she was he'd taken the trouble to give her a day and night in Paris. Her mother wasn't here, so she was as free and unchaperoned as Marie. As she'd been in America. It was a heady sensation. Duty and protocol could be suspended. She was free to do whatever she wished with no one the wiser, and no one watching to see if she made a mistake.

Without the connection to royalty, she had much more freedom. Why hadn't she realized that before?

"I get the pleasure of your company. Don't be so suspicious, Clarissa."

She watched him walk down the hall to his room four doors down. Closing her door, she surveyed the suite he'd obtained for her. Was she being suspicious when she didn't need to be? Or was he trying to lull her into a false sense of security?

And then—what? Pounce?

Jake was hardly the type to pounce. He was more the seductive type, woo a woman and ease her into doing exactly what he wanted.

She'd have to be on her guard.

Unless she wanted what he wanted.

Clarissa crossed to the window and gazed out over the Parisian cityscape. Her thoughts were in turmoil. She didn't know exactly what she wanted. When she was with Jake, she enjoyed every moment. But when they were apart, doubts and worries rose.

She shook off her pensiveness and turned when the bellman brought her luggage. She'd unpack and go spend a day out of time in Paris with her reluctant prince. She'd forget the future, forget his plans to leave. Forget the attraction she couldn't seem to help feeling so strongly when around him—or even just thinking about him. She promised herself a day for pure enjoyment. Time enough tomorrow to face reality.

It was a perfect spring day. The sky was a cloudless blue, the air soft and scented with the fragrances only found in Paris. When Jake came to her door, Clarissa knew how Marie felt as she had almost danced out of the hotel—giddy with excitement. Clarissa felt the same. And when his eyes lighted up at the sight of her, she felt a warm glow. It was heady stuff.

They had café au lait at a pavement café, wandered through Montmartre, viewed the outside of Notre Dame, and strolled along the Left Bank, studying the paintings in progress, commenting, even arguing over which artist was the most likely to become famous and which might as well hang up their brushes and forget it.

They spoke in English and she hoped a time or two the artists in question didn't understand the language. Apparently not, since there was no reaction to some of the comments Jake threw out.

Long before the sun began to set, she knew it had been a perfect day. They laughed, argued and found several things in common—especially a liking for Impressionist art. Her day was proving the best she'd ever spent.

When they walked along crowded streets, he tucked her hand in the crook of his arm, covering it with his fingers. When they crossed a busy street, his arm across her shoulders made her feel cherished and protected. When they laughed, he'd stop and steal a quick kiss, leaving her breathless and longing for more.

Once when she'd said something about Marique, he'd covered her lips with his finger and shook his head.

"Today it's Jake and Clarissa. No duties, obligations, family ties or old regrets. Just you and me, babe."

Paris had never looked so magical. The old buildings took on a romantic glow. The river shone in the sunlight, sparkling as if covered in diamonds.

The shops held little appeal for them, except to spark another discussion. And throughout the afternoon, she learned more about Jake—every bit tucked away to treasure later when he'd gone.

The only poignant note was the growing awareness she began to admit that there was something special about him. Something she wanted in her life—and knew she could never have.

Clarissa was tempted to tell Jake she couldn't go to dinner with him. By the time she was dressed, she dreaded the evening. Their day had been so perfect she was afraid to tempt fate by extending it.

Yet the thought of cutting short their time was unbearable. She was ready when he knocked.

"You look beautiful," he said when she opened the door.

"Thank you." She wanted to return the compliment. He looked sexy and utterly masculine in his dark suit and snowy-white shirt. She remembered him at the construction site, wearing only jeans, and her breath caught. No matter what he wore, or didn't, he looked terrific.

"Marie called and left a message—no trouble so far," he said as he escorted her toward the elevator.

"I hope she's having fun. She has led a very restricted life. She's quite a few years younger than Philippe was. I think they didn't expect to have another child and were so delighted when she was born."

"So they wrap her up and keep her safe?" Jake asked.

"Something like that. Wouldn't you want your children to be safe?"

"There's safe and there's smothering. Children need to explore to discover where they fit in the world. Take advantage of any opportunities to expand their horizons.''

"What were you like as a child?'' she asked. The lift arrived and she was pleased to see they'd be the only occupants.

"Wild and restless.''

"Uh-oh. The LeBlanc tendency. A hellion in the making!''

"But only when I was small. By the time I was a teenager, I held down part-time jobs to help out financially. No time to be wild.''

"Now?''

"Now I'm set in my ways.''

She laughed softly. "You sound like you're a hundred.''

He slanted a look at her and Clarissa caught her breath. Just when she thought she was getting used to the man, a mere look would jump-start her heart and turn her bones to pudding.

Dinner proved lighthearted and fun. They discussed American movies they'd both seen and books that had international acclaim, trying to ascertain what made them liked by different cultures.

The music was seductive and sultry. He held her too close, but she didn't complain. The rhythm was slow, enabling them to do little more than move in place. But pressed up against Jake, Clarissa could feel every hard plane and muscle. Closing her eyes, she ignored the rest of the patrons, and gave herself up to the music, and the delight of being held in Jake's arms. She was glad she'd come. Wished the evening could go on forever.

Somewhere in the middle of the third dance, she realized she was falling in love with Jake White—despite her constant admonitions to herself to avoid that very thing. A touch of panic struck. She couldn't fall in love with a man who didn't love her. One moreover who lived thousands of miles away and had no intention of moving to her country.

When his breath brushed across her cheek, she held herself rigid, unwilling to bend, to relax. Fearful she'd give away her emotions, she counted the seconds until the music ended and she could step away from him. Distance, that's what she needed. Time away from him to let the infatuation die down.

She could not be falling in love with him!

It was torment to be held in those strong arms and not give in to the longings that swept through her. She wanted him to hold her tightly, kiss her senseless and tell her everything would work out.

But she knew better than most that life didn't offer everything she wanted. She'd been in love with Philippe—but not like this. Not like this constant desire to be with Jake, to learn every aspect of his life, to know his opinions, argue with the ones she didn't agree with. To know his every thought, and to share her own. To learn his touch and taste until they were as close as two people could ever be.

"Are you all right?" Jake asked.

"Fine. A bit tired. We did a lot today. And I think I'm getting a headache."

Oh, please. A headache? Couldn't she think of something more original? But Clarissa was feeling desperate. She needed the sanctity of her room.

"Shall we return to the hotel?"

"That might be best," she said.

He stopped in the middle of the dance floor and tipped up her chin, gazing into her eyes. Clarissa felt the heat sweep up into her cheeks. His dark eyes seemed to peer right through her. Did he recognize the lie?

"I'm sorry you're not feeling one hundred percent. We'll leave immediately."

Contrarily, she didn't want the evening to end. She could almost count the hours until he would be leaving for good. How could she cut short the only time she'd have with him?

True to his word, he quickly summoned the check, paid and escorted her outside. In only seconds a cab had been obtained and whisked them through the streets.

The lift was crowded when they stepped inside. And many people remained when they reached their floor. The lack of privacy should have been welcomed.

Jake took her key when she retrieved it from her purse and opened her door for her, dropping the key in her hand.

"I enjoyed today," he said.

"I did, too. It was—" He'd think she was silly if she said magical. But it had been. "—quite wonderful. Thank you." She smiled, hoping he'd kiss her once again. Wondering if she dare kiss him. She swayed just a bit closer. How blatant should she be?

"We'll leave around four tomorrow afternoon. That gives you some time to shop if you wish," he said, checking his watch. "I have a business associate arriving in the morning, so I'll be tied up. Leave a message if you need something and I'm not here."

"Business associate?" It was the first she'd heard of it. "From Los Angeles?"

He nodded.

"Coming to Paris to meet with you?"

"I've put out some feelers to a resort capitalist I know. He's interested in seeing Marique. If he likes what I have to say tomorrow, he'll be coming to Marique with us in the afternoon."

"To build a resort?" Clarissa felt as if she'd missed her cue somewhere. She wanted Jake to kiss her, he was thinking about business!

"If he thinks it looks promising. It would be a good thing—boost the tourist trade. Get to bed. I hope your headache is gone soon."

He turned and walked down the hall toward his room. Clarissa watched, but he never looked back.

Slowly she closed her own door, confused anew by the man. He wanted nothing to do with Marique—yet was coordinating a possible new resort which would create new jobs, and boost the economy. He'd given her name to two venture capitalists who might wish to invest in her fledgling concern. Again, aiding the people of Marique. And the suggestions he'd made at the market—while not earth-shattering, had been helpful.

What else was the man doing? For someone not interested, he sure did a lot.

Jake sent word to Marie for her and Clarissa to meet him in the lobby at three instead of the agreed time of four. He had a successful appointment with Hugh Cartier who was anxious to see Marique. They had run late on their meeting and Jake wanted to return to the little country nestled in the Pyrenees in time for Hugh to get a good overview before dark.

When the two women came down in the lifts, he wryly noticed he had eyes only for Clarissa. He regretted their early ending to their date last night. He wished they could have spent today together as they had yesterday. But he'd needed to meet with Hugh.

Would he and Clarissa ever have another day together? Time was running out. Before long, he'd be back in L.A. and in the midst of negotiations, troubleshooting and scoping out new projects. She'd be back marketing her soap, and maybe expanding the business if the venture capitalists came through. Would she ever come to the States on business?

Introductions were made and the four headed for the airport. Hugh was in his mid-fifties, and looked forty. He and Jake had been friends for a long time—since Jake had build the Cartier's house in Malibu a number of years ago.

"Came as quite a surprise to have Jake here call me about a ground-floor opportunity," Hugh said as the limousine pulled away from the hotel. "Not many things like this left these days. All the good spots have been built on. I should know, I built on plenty of them."

"I didn't know Marique would be considered a desirable destination," Clarissa said.

"We can go two ways," Hugh said. "Either a high-class resort with skiing, hot tubs, and classy acts in the cabarets, or low-key to draw in families. Hell, I may build two resorts, one of each, if the deal is as good as Jake says it is. Property values low, available labor, and gorgeous scenery.''

''You'll see for yourself,'' Jake said lazily. He hadn't taken his eyes off Clarissa. What did she think of the plan? He hadn't mentioned it to anyone, in case it didn't pan out. It still was in the early planning stage. Hugh had a lot of research to do before committing his company to the venture. But Jake was moving fast and wanted a firm deal as soon as he could get it. If Hugh stalled, he'd mention it to some other major firms. And the older man knew that.

The economy of Marique was stagnant. The wool industry would not supply sufficient growth for future needs. By bringing in some fresh ideas and capital, the economy could grow in new directions.

He didn't know what his grandfather would say when he found out. But Jake had done his own homework, working with the ministers and having his own personal assistant back in Los Angeles research climate, demographics, laws and restrictions. The country would be perfect, as Hugh had said, for either kind of resort—or both.

''Do you live in Los Angeles?'' Marie asked.

''Malibu, but it's just a stone's throw from L.A. Ever been there?'' Hugh replied, smiling at her.

''Not yet, but I'm heading that way soon. I'll be staying for a few weeks at Jake's apartment.''

Clarissa looked at her in surprise, her glance then flying to Jake.

He nodded.

Much as Jake wanted to sit with Clarissa on the airplane, he resisted the urge and sat beside Hugh, letting his guest have a window seat that would give a good view of Marique when they approached. They continued their discussion about the resort, Jake with only half attention. He tried to listen to Marie and Clarissa's conversation at the same time—with poor results.

When they landed, Hugh was beaming. "Perfect so far. I don't think you've steered me wrong here, Jake. I can't wait to see the locations you considered."

"Actually there are parts of the country I haven't seen yet. We can explore the western section together."

"I can go with you and answer any questions you might have," Marie volunteered. "I want to take a more active role in things concerning Marique."

"Good idea. Clarissa, how about you?"

"I wish I could, but I have commitments tomorrow. Another time perhaps?" she said, taken aback at how fast things seemed to be moving. A tycoon's way, she thought wryly, wishing Jake had moved as quickly in cementing their friendship. Or more.

Was she reading more into their relationship than really was there? Wishful thinking, she mused, sitting back and letting the conversation swirl around her.

She was surprised at how left out she felt when dropped at her home. Watching the others sparking ideas for different locales and how to easily accommodate a large influx of tourists made her wish to be a part of the discussion.

Duty called, however. She'd neglected her own involvement in her fledgling business while dealing with Jake. She needed to fulfill her own commitments before making more.

But she wished she could be a part of their schemes. If nothing else, Jake would most likely keep in touch to see how the resort progressed. He might even come to visit it from time to time.

The next afternoon Clarissa answered a summons from Gustine. They had tea together and she turned aside the inquisition as best she was able. Gustine wanted to know every detail of their visit to Paris and was not particularly pleased with Clarissa's vague responses.

"How are the renovations going on the quarters for Jean-Antoine?" Gustine asked, finally giving up on trying to glean further information on the Parisian trip.

Clarissa sipped her tea, stalling. Why did Gustine insist on calling him Jean-Antoine when everyone else called him Jake? As a courtesy to his title? Or to annoy him? The latter most likely.

"Slowly." Like in dead stop.

"It must be difficult. I don't know what His Majesty was thinking. How are you to be expected to help him furnish his home when you and Philippe should have had your own quarters and been living in marital bliss by now! It's unconscionable, I'd say."

Clarissa daintily bit into a petit four and shrugged. She didn't want to get into a discussion with Gustine about that. Or reveal the fact she wasn't at all sure that even if Philippe had lived they would have been married by now.

In fact, it was difficult to even envision being married to him. Jake filled her thoughts. With his cousin, she would have been left behind when Philippe traveled. She had always known that, though she had tried to convince herself differently.

She would never have that with Jake. If he went somewhere, he'd want to take the woman he loved with him.

The woman he loved. Her heart flipped over just imagining herself as that person. He was attentive to a stranger, how attentive would he be to family members he cared about?

Look at how he'd helped Marie. She was blossoming beyond what Clarissa had ever thought possible.

Imagine how a woman he loved would be lavished with attention. And caring. And love.

"Clarissa!"

She blinked and looked at Gustine. "I beg your pardon. My mind wandered a moment."

"I don't wonder. What with all that's going on and the reception this Saturday. His Majesty could have waited on that," she said waspishly.

"He is anxious to introduce Jake to all and sundry. To have the people know there is an heir and the succession is assured." And once the reception was over, did Jake plan to leave?

Clarissa couldn't stop things from unfolding, but she could let His Majesty know Jake's plans. At least spare him the humiliation of his departure.

"Excuse me, Gustine. Thank you for inviting me to tea. But there's something I really need to do."

Clarissa had been in and out of the palace for several years, but she had never sought an audience with the king before. She wasn't sure of her reception, but she had to try.

It proved to be remarkably easy.

"Hello, Clarissa. You wished to see me?" the king said when she was ushered into his office.

She glanced around quickly, surprised to find it looked like any businessman's office. Two phones were on the desk. A computer sat to one side. A small, neat pile of folders were stacked on the right edge.

She nodded and sat when he indicated she should.

"Thank you for seeing me, Your Majesty."

"I think we can dispense with formality when we are alone. I had hopes you'd one day be my granddaughter and present me with another generation."

Clarissa was touched by his words. "I had hopes of that, as well. I still miss Philippe."

"One wonders, however, how effective a king he would have made."

Clarissa blinked. She had thought she was the only one with such thoughts.

"But I suspect you didn't come to reminisce or speculate about Philippe."

"No, I came about Jake. I mean, His Royal Highness, Jean-Antoine."

"He seems to prefer Jake," the older man said.

"I may be overstepping bounds, but I think you ought to know I think Jake plans to return to America immediately after the reception. He has never planned to stay in Marique.''

The king was silent for a moment, then seemed to wilt slightly before her eyes.

''I feared something would prevent the succession. He said often enough in the beginning he wasn't going to stay. I ignored it, thinking once he saw how things were— Well, it wasn't enough.''

''He doesn't care about the succession. He cares about family!'' she said heatedly.

''Ah, and his let him down.''

She didn't have to agree, the truth was obvious.

''I should not have involved you in family problems,'' the king said gently.

''I am always happy to be of service however you best think I can serve,'' she replied formally, wishing there was something she could do to change the sadness that had enveloped the older man.

''His quarters? Have you done anything for them?''

She shook her head. ''I thought it pointless.''

''Perhaps it is. But I would have you draft some preliminary plans. You know my grandson better than I do.''

''Are any of the furniture or decorations from Joseph's time around? I asked Gustine, but she wasn't certain.''

The king nodded. ''I'll instruct Stephan to give you whatever assistance you need. Who knows, maybe having a place to call his own in Marique will entice him back someday.''

"I hope so, Your Majesty." Clarissa rose. "I'm sorry to be the bearer of bad news."

"Thank you for alerting me. It will make things easier when he goes."

Standing in indecision in the hallway after she left, Clarissa wished she could knock their stubborn heads together. The two men might never develop close feelings, but they were family and should work to heal the breach!

She picked up a notepad from the secretary's desk and headed to the apartments set aside for Jake. The door wasn't locked. Entering, she could almost imagine she heard the echo of laughter and music. From what Philippe had told her, Joseph, Prince of Marique, had been fun-loving, happy and always into mischief. Another hell-raiser. Would Jake have developed the same tendencies had he been brought up in luxury instead of having to make his own way in the world?

Not in the same way, of that she was sure.

She wandered down the hall, peering into the rooms, wondering if she should sketch some preliminary plans. Would it be futile? Or if she refurbished the rooms like his father had had them, would Jake be pleased?

Entering what had once been the master bedroom, she went to the windows and pulled back the curtains. A cloud of dust descended and she stepped back quickly. The windows needed cleaning, and the curtains needed to be replaced.

The view was magnificent. She looked over the formal gardens, beyond to the maze, remembering that first night.

"Clarissa?"

She turned slowly, not surprised to see Jake. Had she heard something? Or was this part of a dream?

"Yes?"

"What are you doing here?"

"Just dreaming."

"Dreaming?"

"Of what the apartment could be like. I asked about furniture and decorations from your father. There are some still about. If we locate them, we could furnish the place close to how he had it. Would that make a difference?"

"To what?" Jake stepped inside.

"To your staying?"

He shook his head. Stepped closer. Slowly he reached out and drew her into his arms. "Come with me when I leave."

CHAPTER NINE

His mouth closed over hers and he drew her tightly against him. His lips were warm and demanding. In the space of a heartbeat, reality faded and the magic they'd found in Paris swept through her again.

Clarissa gave herself up to his embrace, delighting in the sensations that coursed through her. In the heat that blossomed and built. The pulsing excitement had her feeling more like a woman than anything else in her life.

His tongue traced the line of her lips and she opened for him. Time spun out of control. Faster, slower, stopped. A kaleidoscope of colors danced behind her lids as she sought more and more from his embrace.

Her fingers tangled in his dark hair, relishing the thickness and warmth. Her breasts pressed against his hard chest, swelling with desire as the kiss went on and on. Clothes were an encumbrance. She wanted to feel more of him. To touch his bronzed skin covering the hardened muscles of his chest. To relish the heat of his body as she learned every inch.

His own fingers threaded through her hair, moving her head to better deepen the kiss. He kissed as if he couldn't get enough. As if she were drink to a thirsty man, or bread to one starving.

She couldn't think, couldn't reason. Could do nothing but feel.

Come with him? At this point she'd follow him to the ends of the earth.

His hand moved to her neck, gently massaging. When he moved to slip beneath the edge of her collar, she made no protest. His fingertips were warm, tracing fire and ice along her skin.

A button slipped free, then another. His hand was moving against her, caressing, driving her wild.

Another button was unfastened and his hand gently cupped a breast. The shock of surprise went to her toes.

When his thumb brushed her nipple, her knees went weak. She made a sound deep in her throat—half moan, half purr.

Slowly they sank to the floor. She didn't even notice the hardwood, she was lost in a cloud of exquisite passion. The only reality in time and space was Jake.

She traced the strength of his shoulders. Fumbling, she slipped her hands beneath his shirt, shivering in delight at the heat of his body.

With one swift movement, he whipped the shirt over his head and tossed it aside. Opening the bodice of her dress the rest of the way, he pulled back enough to look at her.

"You are so beautiful. I want you, Clarissa."

She smiled lazily, but didn't say anything. Talk about the obvious.

When she didn't protest, he unfastened her bra and bared her breasts.

"You are so beautiful." The words were repeated in a half whisper, as if in awe.

She felt beautiful—more so than ever before.

He drew her closer, so her breasts were pressed against the strength of his chest. She closed her eyes in bliss. She'd never done this before. What had she been missing?

His mouth claimed hers again and she wrapped her arms around him, holding on as if to never let go.

"Jake?"

They stopped, frozen as the voice called again from the main salon. It was the king.

Jake stood up in one swift move, pulling Clarissa with him. Releasing her, he looked around for his shirt. He snatched it up, shook it once and pulled it on, tucking it into his trousers as he started for the hall.

Clarissa couldn't move. She hastily pulled her dress closed, licked her lips, tasting him still, feeling they were slightly swollen. Shock held her immobile for a long moment. Then she exploded into action. She couldn't be caught like this! Not by the king. Not by anyone!

She scrambled to refasten her bra, then her dress, brushing off the dust as best she could.

Jake had reached the salon. She could hear the murmur of voices. Finger-brushing her hair, she wished there was a mirror somewhere.

Clarissa glanced down. As far as she could tell, she looked okay. Picking up her notepad, she followed slowly. She hoped she didn't look as disheveled and just-made-love-to as she felt. Her heart pounded, her skin seemed too tight. What if they'd been caught? She shivered at the horror. She didn't even want to go there in her mind!

She paused before bursting into the salon when she

heard the king speak. Leaning against the wall, she wondered if maybe she could escape detection. She should have waited in the bedroom, but after what had happened, she didn't dare risk being discovered there. Yet she hesitated to intrude.

No one but Jake knew she was here. It would be best if she left it that way!

"You wanted to see me?" The hard tone was Jake's.

"One of the footmen told me he'd seen you come this way. How do you like the apartment?"

"As with everything in the palace, it is superb."

"Your father chose this one himself when he was eighteen."

Clarissa heard footsteps moving toward the windows. "I didn't realize what neglect would do to the place. Your grandmother would have grieved. I'll have it cleaned immediately."

Jake remained silent. The quiet stretched out so long Clarissa wondered if she should join them. Then the king began to speak.

"When you get to be an old man, you begin to think about decisions made when younger. You won't believe it, but Joseph was my favorite son. Not that a father is supposed to have a favorite. Michael was a good man. And I miss him every day. But he was not the flamboyant daredevil your father was. And he didn't have Joseph's flare for laughter. God, I've missed him!"

"You show favoritism by repudiation?" Jake said skeptically.

"No. I was trying to control my brash and reckless son. I had hoped the threat of cutting him off from family and fortune would curb his extravagances, rein in his impetuosity. I was trying to protect my beloved son from his own recklessness.''

''It always sounded to me as if it spurred him on to greater risks, from what my mother said.''

''I should have trusted his judgment. Let him get the wildness out of his system. Hindsight leads me to believe he would have returned home and taken his rightful place. I also should have trusted he would spot a gold digger a mile away and steer clear. I ought to have given him that trust and acknowledged he had the right to live his life as he wished. To marry where he wished.''

''He did anyway.''

''We grieved so the day we learned of his death.''

The shuffle of footsteps had Clarissa wondering what they were doing. Were they turning to face each other? She dare not peek around the corner to see, but wished she knew if Jake was at least listening. Tears filled her eyes at the sorrow in the king's voice. He was a father still grieving for a lost child.

''Pride and stubbornness are traits to watch out for,'' the king continued. ''Had I not both in abundance, I might have been more open about meeting your mother. To meeting you as a child. I offer you my sincerest apologies for the past. If I could change it today, I would.''

Say something! Clarissa willed. But Jake remained silent.

''I understand you'll be leaving after the reception this weekend.''

''Clarissa?'' Jake guessed.

''She thought I should know. I'm sorry. I had hoped

even at this late date that we could find some common ground. However, unless you formally repudiate the crown, it will still be yours once I'm gone. Give some thought to taking it. It has been in our family many generations.''

"If I don't want it?"

"The rules of succession are murky. Never in the entire history of our family's rule have we faced not having a male heir. I'm sure the ministers and lawyers will determine the rightful course. But I ask you not to let my mistakes of the past alter the future. Even if you wait until I'm gone, think of your heritage carefully before turning away.''

"Maybe Marie should succeed you. She's been raised here, knows the people and what the country needs,'' Jake said.

"It's possible. She's a direct descendant. We've never had a ruling queen before. Interesting thought.''

Clarissa heard slow footsteps. They stopped.

"Before I forget. The reason I came. This is for you. It was your father's. I would say it would give me pleasure to see you wear it at the reception, but that would probably insure you didn't. It's yours to do with as you wish.''

The steps came closer, passed by as the king left the apartment.

Clarissa stayed where she was for a moment, then stepped around the corner into the large room.

"Had to tell, huh?'' Jake said, turning to face her. In his hand, a medallion on a wide ribbon. It was hard to determine from his expression whether he was angry or not.

"Yes, I did. I would not see anyone deliberately hurt and what you planned would have been devastating."

"He seems to be holding up well enough."

"He's seen more turmoil and heartache in his lifetime than you'll probably ever see. Of course he holds up well, he's our king."

Jake glanced at the medallion. Clarissa stepped closer and peered at it as it sat on Jake's palm.

"It's the official state seal—a medallion for a prince. Which you are," she said softly. "It's worn with formal attire at receptions and state dinners."

"He said it was my father's."

"I heard. I heard all he said and feel sad at how things turned out. Do you think if your father had not been killed so young they would have made up? Your father could have come home and brought you and your mother. Things would have been so different."

"Who knows? The past can't be changed."

"But the future could be," Clarissa said softly.

He closed his fist around the medallion and looked at her, his eyes glittering.

"Are you coming to L.A. with me when I go?"

No words of love or devotion. No expression of feeling or sentiment. Simply come with him. Why? As a further slap in the face to the king? For a wild, passionate affair? Of that she had no doubt it would be.

To what end?

She shook her head. "My place is here. My home is here. There's nothing for me in Los Angeles."

"I live there."

"So you do."

"I thought..." He looked away. "Never mind. It's obvious where your loyalties lie."

"Why did you come here today? To these quarters? Where's Hugh?"

"It's early in California. He wanted to get on the phone with some of his partners and discuss the sites we looked at today before they got going on other things."

"So he likes them?"

"He's trying to play the cards close to his chest, but, yeah, he likes them. And if we can make some concessions, I bet he'll break ground by next spring."

"Will your construction firm build the hotel?"

Jake shook his head. "We're not international."

"You could open a branch here in Marique."

"Why would I want to do that?"

"To make sure you got to build the resort, to ensure it's just as you envision it. You have a tie to this country whether or not you want to admit it."

"Jean-Antoine?" Gustine opened the door and looked inside. Satisfied her target was in sight, she entered.

"This place is worse than Grand Central Station," Jake muttered.

Gustine looked closely at Clarissa and sniffed. "You knew all along this man was not planning to stay. Why not tell us at the beginning? You are like a daughter to me. If Philippe hadn't died, you would be my daughter-in-law by now. To think you'd turn on your own family for an outsider."

"I don't think of Jake as an outsider," Clarissa murmured. "If anyone is, it's I."

"Nonsense. You're family. Even the king thinks so."

Gustine turned her sharp gaze on her nephew. "And you, what do you think you're doing talking about returning to America? We had enough of that when you first arrived. That's merely your stubborn, prideful LeBlanc tendencies showing. Being a prince is a much better choice than a carpenter. Your place is here. Your grandfather isn't going to live forever, you know. You have a lot to learn before taking the reins of the government."

"If I had been contacted before now, maybe I would have had a chance to learn more."

"Fst," she waved a hand as if clearing the air. "You're here now. It's more than my boy is. Take advantage of the time you have with His Majesty. Life can be extinguished in a heartbeat."

Clarissa reached out and touched Jake, hoping to stem any outrageous comment he might make. It had taken a lot for Gustine to come to ask him to stay. She recognized that, even if he didn't.

Jake glanced at her, his expression impassive. She wished she could tell what he was thinking.

"You surprise me, Aunt," he said, "I believe your feelings toward me have been less than—warm."

Gustine drew herself up regal in bearing as befitted a woman who had been crown princess for more than two decades. "Perhaps in my zeal to offer suggestions for improvements I have come across as a bit stern. It has always been my intention to do my best for the country.

You are the next in line for succession. If I can help ensure you will be a great king, I know my duty.''

Jake's eyes twinkled. Clarissa turned away so she wouldn't be tempted to smile. Gustine's heart was in the right place, even if her manner was off. It couldn't be easy after losing her own son, to see another take his place. But, as with Clarissa, she knew her duty.

''I'll take it under advisement,'' Jake said.

Gustine nodded. She looked at Clarissa. ''I see you are continuing to work on the apartment despite what he says.''

Clarissa nodded, clutching the notepad, thankful she'd brought it with her. She hoped Gustine didn't look too closely, afraid she'd guess what she and Jake had been doing before the king arrived.

''Do a good job.'' Gustine nodded to both and turned to leave.

Silence engulfed the room as Clarissa and Jake watched her departure.

When the door closed behind her, Clarissa looked at him.

''You never said why you came here.''

''You didn't say why you are here. Not still working on a decorating plan, I take it.''

She shrugged. ''I had some ideas. So I wandered through to see if they'd work.''

''Today's Thursday. The reception is Saturday and I leave on Sunday. Why spend time on a fruitless task?''

She shrugged. ''Are you and Hugh going to check out other sites or do you think he'll settle for one of the ones you already showed him?''

"Actually, he and Marie are going to the western area in the morning and won't return until Saturday afternoon. She has a couple of places she thought he ought to see before making a final decision."

"But you aren't going?"

Jake shook his head. "I have more meetings with the ministers. Then I want to drive around some more, on my own."

"Saying goodbye?"

He raised an eyebrow. "Don't attribute me with sentiments I don't have. It's a new place, I want to see it before I leave."

A perfunctory knock came on the door, then it was opened.

"Beg pardon, Your Highness." One of the footmen stood in the opening. "Mr. Cartier was looking for you."

"This place *is* worse than Grand Central Station," Jake muttered. "Tell him I'll be right there."

Clarissa hugged the notepad, looking at him, wishing there was something she could say. She wished he'd take her in his arms again. Kiss her, make love to her.

But he was already moving toward the door. Away. And after the reception, he'd be going for good. Should she have taken him up on his invitation? Could she have lived in Los Angeles?

By early afternoon the next day, Jake was ready to toss in the towel. He'd met with various ministers that morning. Obviously the king had prepped them. Their not-so-subtle hints about his staying wore on his nerves. He'd gone through the motions, but chafed at the charade. He wasn't staying, why pretend?

By noon he'd thanked them for their insights and dismissed them one and all.

Heading for his room, he wondered what he was doing staying for the reception. It gave rise to false expectations. Jake was a straight shooter. He didn't manipulate facts to make deals, didn't sugarcoat bad news in business. Why go through the motions here when he knew he was leaving?

To appease his grandfather?

The thought struck him with surprise. He didn't want to do anything to appease the old man. He'd made his bed, let him lie on it.

Jeremy waited in his quarters.

"I thought you'd be off doing something."

"Like what, sir?" he asked, automatically reaching to assist Jake with removing his suit jacket.

"I was supposed to be tied up all day in meetings. How did you know I'd be returning earlier?"

Jeremy smiled slightly. "It's my job to know."

Jake loosened his tie. "I'm leaving Sunday."

Jeremy dipped his head once in acknowledgment. "Will you be requiring my services in Los Angeles?"

Jake gave a short laugh. "I doubt it. I've managed for thirty-two years on my own, I think I can manage on my own again once I return home."

"Then perhaps I can act for you here. Send reports on how His Majesty is doing, news of your aunt and cousin."

"That won't be necessary. Marie is coming to visit me in L.A."

"I'm sure you'll show her a good time, sir." Jeremy followed Jake into the bedroom.

"I can take it from here," Jake grumbled. He still didn't like the older man hovering around.

"If I might suggest, perhaps a change of scenery would aid you in making a proper decision."

"Such as?" He knew what Jeremy's proper decision would be. The same as Gustine's, Marie's, Clarissa's and the king's. Stay in Marique.

"Belle Terrace. It's very popular. The view is spectacular. It is a short drive up the mountain, then there's a tram to the top. There are several footpaths for walks. I don't believe you've seen the city from its vantage point."

"Maybe."

"I'll arrange for the car to be brought 'round." Jeremy bowed slightly and left the room. Jake took off his tie and shirt. What the hell, why not? He could use some fresh air.

And a companion.

A half hour later he stopped at Clarissa's place. Climbing the three stairs to her front door, he rang the bell. It took her several minutes to answer. So long, he began to wonder if she were home.

"Jake. I didn't expect to see you. Is there something wrong?"

"You only expect to see me if something is wrong?"

She shook her head. "Come in."

"Are you in the middle of something?"

"I was on the phone with Paulette about a shipment of wrappers for the soap that has been delayed. It will hold things up another day. Frustrating, but not earthshaking."

He stepped inside.

"You look like you did in L.A.," she murmured, taking in his jeans and chambray shirt with the sleeves rolled above his forearms.

"I'm going hiking. Change and come with me."

He saw the hesitation, knew she wanted to refuse. Wickedly, he added, "As a royal command, I order you to accompany me to Belle Terrace."

Her gaze met his. Was there a hint of amusement in her eyes? For once he couldn't read her expression.

"Your wish is my command."

"Wear your jeans."

"Your wish—"

"I get the point. Just hurry."

"No rock climbing, just a hike?"

"Just walking along mountain trails. Nothing daring at all. I'm not the wild and daring adventurer my cousin was."

"You seem pretty adventurous to me."

"Ah, but you've led a sheltered life."

No one wants to be told they led a sheltered life—it implied they were unsophisticated and naive.

"Not so sheltered," she murmured, fired up to prove him wrong. The only question was—how?

Time was winding down. In two days he planned to return to L.A. He had today to see some more of the country and spend time with Clarissa. Tomorrow evening was the reception to meet those the king deemed persons of rank. Jake had included a few of his own choices to the invitation list—one of the stall owners from La Rouchere, two of the primary soap manufacturers Clarissa had introduced him to, and the men who owned the two properties Hugh liked.

He was aware of the fleeting moments. He longed to lean down the few inches that separated them and brush a kiss across her lips. But yesterday's kiss had gotten out of control. Clarissa wasn't one to fool around, or indulge in a one-night stand. He respected her too much to dishonor her in such a way.

And she'd made it clear by her refusal to visit him in Los Angeles that she didn't want any connection.

But the temptation was strong to pick up where they left off yesterday and see where it led.

By midafternoon when they reached the tram, the platform was almost deserted. Waiting for the next tram, Jake had Clarissa point out the places of interest they could see from this vantage point. When the tram arrived, they were joined by two other couples, one of whom obviously recognized him. They whispered between themselves, then said something softly to the other couple.

Jake was getting used to being stared at. He smiled and nodded.

Clarissa watched him. When he looked at her, she smiled warmly. It was all he could do to refrain from taking her in his arms and kissing her.

They waited for the others to disembark and head for the viewing platform before they left the tram.

"Want to walk for a bit first? There are other viewing platforms," Clarissa suggested.

"Lead on."

They walked in silence for a little while, then Clarissa said, "You are good with strangers. Their staring doesn't seem to bother you."

"Doesn't matter if it does or doesn't, they're going to do it. Most of the people I've met in Marique are friendly."

"And thrilled to meet their prince."

"Don't start."

"You're right, of course. Nothing I can say will make a difference. Would your mother have approved of your plan?"

Jake reached the next viewing platform and walked to the edge. The view was perfect. Rugged mountain peaks seemed to encircle a huge valley in which the capital was nestled. The green spread out below was rich and deep, complimented by the dark blue cloudless sky. The air was fresh and cool.

"My mother wanted nothing more than for me to come to Marique and take my rightful place. But I wouldn't have come without her and you know the views of the king and Aunt Gustine. The entire family for all I know."

"Philippe talked about looking you up one time," she murmured.

"Why?"

"Just to meet his cousin. But he was great for procrastinating, and I guess he ran out of time."

"What will you do now? Develop your soap business?"

"Yes. I've already heard from one of the names you gave me. The talk proved enlightening. I'm excited about the possibilities."

"No family, no bunch of kids running around?"

When she didn't reply, he looked at her, startled to see tears in her eyes. He could have kicked himself. He hadn't meant to make her cry. Of course she still missed his cousin. Was still in love with a man he'd never met. She'd said in L.A. that she wasn't looking to fall in love again. A one-man woman, that was Clarissa.

"Come on, let's see those other views before it gets too late."

For him it was already too late.

CHAPTER TEN

SATURDAY morning Jake kept to his rooms. Marie was still in the western part of the country, showing Hugh other sites. He missed her at breakfast. Odd how quickly things could change. He'd eaten breakfast alone since his mother died, except for a few days with Marie, and he liked the company.

He had no meeting scheduled that day, as if everyone needed to rest up for the reception that evening. Maybe his grandfather needed to rest. He was eighty-four. Not a young man.

Jake headed for the rogue's gallery, as he called the hallway with the portraits of the former kings and queens of Marique. Slowly he studied them, starting with his grandfather when he'd been a young man. There was a spark in his eyes Jake had never seen. Had losing his sons and wife extinguished it? Or was it a trick of light?

He gazed at the portrait of his grandmother as a young woman, wondering how she'd felt to become queen. If she'd loved her husband, or loved the title more. Something to think about when a king chose a mate, he thought.

Others whom he didn't know gazed impassively down at him as he walked along the corridor. Jewels and rich gowns adorned the women. Sometimes a beard or mustache adorned the men. Hair worn short, queued, powdered. Garments ranging from somber black to colorful brocades. There were not enough portraits to cover six hundred years, but there were obviously enough to go back three hundred at least.

Quite a change from the small apartments he and his mother had shared in the poorer section of Las Vegas, Nevada. Abruptly, he turned and left. He'd check out the maze again, see the gardens in daylight and maybe have Jeremy get started packing.

He refused to speculate about the next portrait to go on the wall. Would it be Marie in full regalia? Or some distant male cousin he didn't even know about? Not the direct line, but a collateral branch of the family?

Maybe he would have Jeremy send him a note from time to time—just to keep him up on what was happening.

The reception started at seven. Promptly at six-fifty, Jake appeared in the antechamber his grandfather had designated for the family to meet. Gustine was already there, splendid in a ball gown of silver, with diamonds discreetly at her neck and ears. Her hair had been coifed in a formal style and she looked regal and unapproachable.

Jake had worn formal tails and a snowy-white cravat and cummerbund. Despite what his grandfather had thought, Jake wore the medallion—to honor his father.

His grandfather arrived immediately behind him— also wearing tails, with a band across his chest resplendent with medals and another medallion. His carriage was erect, his demeanor calm.

If he was upset his only grandson was leaving in the

morning, turning his back on all he had to offer, he gave no sign.

Marie hurried into the room, breathless. "Sorry I'm late. But I'm not really late, it doesn't start for another few minutes."

"We gather beforehand to make sure we are not tardy," her mother said.

"I'm not." Marie smiled at Jake. "You look terrific. All the women will swoon and hope to catch the eye of an eligible prince."

"Nonsense. Nobody is going to swoon. And everyone here will know the proper methods for a prince to choose a bride."

"And that would entail?" Jake asked.

"A family committee to vet the prospective women," Marie said. She darted a quick look at her grandfather. "And Grandfather makes the final decision."

As he had vetoed Jake's father's choice. Only the family committee had never even met his mother.

"We have other things to think about tonight beside Jake getting married," Gustine said stiffly. "Are you sure a receiving line is a proper way to introduce the prince?"

The king nodded. "Jean-Antoine requested it."

"Instead of the formal curtsies and bows?" Marie asked. "Why didn't I know that? I would have worn more comfortable shoes. I thought we'd be sitting."

"If you had been home in a reasonable time this afternoon, you would have," her mother said. "It's too late now to change, you'll just have to endure."

"Mr. Cartier was so interested in seeing as much as

he could, we ran late. I already explained. And why a receiving line?"

"So your cousin can meet the people face-to-face."

Marie laughed. "That's his democratic upbringing, I imagine."

Jake nodded. He'd been surprised when he'd suggested it that the king had acquiesced. But Jake wasn't one for sitting on a dais and having people bow before him. How would he have handled things if he had decided to remain in Marique? How would an American adjust to a monarchy?

"It's time." The king looked at Jake long and hard. "I hope you remember the people you met tonight had nothing to do with your father's rebellion or my decisions."

Jake inclined his head slightly. Did the king think him so unmannered as to cause a scene? Had his grandfather learned nothing about him in the weeks he'd lived in the palace?

The older man led the way into the huge ballroom where the reception was to take place.

The crystal chandeliers sparkled and shimmered with light. The polished floors reflected the illumination. A string quartet played discreetly at the far corner. Gilt chairs and love seats lined the walls. At the far end, the royal thrones sat in empty splendor.

Just before a footman opened the tall doors, the king took his place to the right, Jake beside him, Gustine and Marie beyond him. At the king's nod, the doors were thrown open and the majordomo announced the first guest.

Forty-five minutes later Jake had serious second thoughts about holding a receiving line. Had the king invited the entire nation? His hand ached from so many handshakes. His cheeks felt permanently locked into a smile, and he hadn't a hope in heaven of keeping half the names straight.

When Clarissa stepped in front of him, he felt a wave of relief.

"Yankee informality?" she asked softly, smiling politely and offering her hand. "No curtsies, no bows? Amazing."

He took her gloved hand and just held it. "How far out of town does the line extend?"

She gave a soft gurgle of laughter and glanced around the room with a practiced eye. "I'd say you are halfway there."

"I may have been too hasty in suggesting this. But how much longer would it have taken to have each couple walk down the aisle and bow?"

"Longer, I expect, but at least you would have been sitting. Oops, I must move along or I'll hold things up."

Someone had warned the guests he spoke no French. They addressed him in English or Spanish. By the time the last of the guests arrived, Jake wanted a drink and a quiet corner. Neither was forthcoming.

The king addressed him stiffly. "I will lead your aunt out in dancing. After we have circled the floor once, you join us with Marie. The others cannot begin until we have observed the formalities," his grandfather said. "Once the dancing has started, you needn't continue if you don't wish. I expect there are many people who knew your father here who will wish to speak to you about him.''

Without a noticeable signal, he let the band know to change tunes and begin a waltz. He and Gustine stepped into the center of the huge room, miraculously cleared.

They danced once around the space. Right on cue, Jake and Marie stepped into the clearing and began to dance.

"Tradition," Marie said. "It's comforting in a way, even though I chafe at it sometimes. At least I know what's expected and what to do. I think I'll feel a bit lost when I visit America.''

"But you'll adapt.''

"Of course. It's what LeBlancs do. Besides, I'll have my big cousin there to lead the way. And it's only a visit. I'll end up coming back home.''

Jake nodded, his gaze skimming around the room.

"Clarissa is to your right, near Mr. Cartier. You can ask her to dance once. To do more would cause comment.''

"I believe between your mother and our grandfather, they covered every minute detail of etiquette Marique style.''

"Is it different from American etiquette?''

"Some of the rules and traditions are. The rest is just good manners—universal in any culture I expect.''

The waltz ended. Marie tucked her hand into the crook of Jake's arm and walked with him toward Clarissa. Before they reached her, however, an elderly couple stopped to speak to Jake. They had known his grandmother and his father.

Marie made a hasty exit and Jake was left alone to fend for himself. Another couple joined them. In a few moments, a man his father's age joined the group. He introduced himself as Claude Monsarot.

Jake listened intently when they spoke of his father, trying to get a fuller picture of the man he'd never known. He kept track of Clarissa even as the others spoke to him. She danced with a tall man who appeared very attentive. Then a short, elderly man. She looked as regal as his aunt. She would have made a perfect princess. Did she regret not marrying before his cousin had died? At least she'd have had the title.

Yet by neither word nor deed had she ever indicated that title was important to her. Even with no chance at it, she continued to be dutifully attentive to her almost mother-in-law and sister-in-law.

More stories about his father were forthcoming. While Jake appreciated the opportunity to learn more about him, he was itching to dance with Clarissa. And to hell with convention, maybe he would take several dances with her.

Only, at the rate he was going, the reception would end before he made it to her side to even ask for one.

Uniformed footmen wove in and out of the crowd, serving fine champagne and wine. One of the antechambers held lavish hors d'oeuvre selections. The doors from that room opened to the gardens.

Jake wondered if he could escape the current group and spirit Clarissa off to the maze. They'd have privacy there! It was his last night in Marique—he wanted at least one dance with her.

And another kiss.

"I have pictures of your father and me when we were younger," Claude said. "I'd be happy to show them to you sometime."

"I'd like to see them." No need to tell the man it was unlikely to happen.

"If he hadn't gone off in such anger, he would have become crowned prince when Prince Michael died. Always was a hothead. A bit of patience and he'd have had what he always wanted."

"My father wanted to inherit the throne?" The thought had never crossed Jake's mind. Joseph had been a younger son, reared from infancy not to expect to succeed to the throne.

"That's what the final fight with his father was about. The stories I could tell—"

"Maybe you should." Jake smiled charmingly to the others in the group, and excused himself and Claude. They strolled outside to the relative privacy of the gardens. Clarissa was forgotten for the moment. Jake wanted to learn what Claude could tell him.

A half hour later they returned to the reception. Jake immediately scanned the ballroom to locate Clarissa. She was in the midst of a group which also held Marie and Hugh. He made his way directly there, smiling politely when people spoke to him, but not slowing his pace. The evening was too short to be sidetracked.

When he joined the group, Clarissa looked at him in surprise.

"Is there something wrong?" she asked.

"If I might excuse Clarissa, I have need of her," he

said to the others. Gripping her arm lightly, he turned her toward the antechamber and the gardens.

"You have need of me?" Clarissa said softly.

"Sounded better than 'I want to spend time with Clarissa and not anyone else,' don't you think?"

"Shh, someone will hear you."

"I understand I only get one dance with you. Should it be now, or later?"

"Whenever you wish," she replied primly.

"So what would happen if we began dancing with this song and I never let you go?"

"The country would never recover from the scandal."

He continued out of the ballroom and through to the garden.

"Only if they could see us."

"What do you mean?"

"If we are in the maze, how many others could find their way to the center?"

She laughed. "Jake, you can't leave the reception. It's in your honor."

"It was for the king."

"In a way. But also to introduce you to the populace."

"I *thought* he'd invited most of the country."

"Nonsense, there are probably no more than three hundred people here tonight. Our population is much larger than that."

They nodded to another couple as Jake led them down one path—the opening to the maze his goal.

"Really, Jake, you can't do this."

"Did you know my father wanted to be king?"

"He did? I didn't know."

"And if he hadn't run off and then gotten himself killed at a young age, he would have made it—since Michael and Philippe died. Instead, he left in a snit, I believe is how Claude put it, when Philippe was born."

"So you would have ended up right where you are today—heir apparent to the throne."

He hesitated a moment, looking at her. "I guess you're right."

"Can't fight fate," she said cheerfully.

They reached the maze and Jake looked around. There were several couples strolling the lighted paths of the garden, but none were near enough to follow them. He stepped to the opening, but Clarissa stopped.

"No. I won't go with you. It's an affront to your grandfather. Despite everything, he doesn't deserve your insulting him in front of his people."

"And having a few moments of privacy is an affront?"

"I suspect we would be gone for more than a few minutes."

He brushed her cheek softly with the backs of his fingers. "I expect so. Would that be so bad? It's my last night. Since you won't come to L.A., I might never see you again."

"You'll know where to find me."

"And you know where I live."

Clarissa couldn't stand this. It was worse than losing Philippe. She had thought she loved her fiancé, and had she never met Jake, she might have gone to her grave believing that.

But after spending this short time with Jake, she knew better. She loved every bit of this infuriating man. She wanted to spend her days and nights with him. To exchange ideas, learn more about how he thought, and of the good he did without even thinking about it.

She didn't approve of his plan to turn his back on his heritage, but she admired his standing up for what he believed, no matter what the cost.

If only—

"I need to say goodbye now, Jake," she said softly, her heart clutching in anguish. She hoped he didn't realize how hard this was for her.

"We haven't had that dance."

"Goodbye, Jake. Have a happy life." She turned and swiftly walked up the path, eyes shimmering with tears.

She had to leave. She had attended the reception, been seen. She'd mingled, danced, laughed. If people thought it odd she left early, they could put it down to heartache caused by the prince. Only she'd know which prince caused her heartache.

The next morning Marie accompanied Jake and Hugh to the airport. She chatted during the short ride, telling Jake over and over her plans to visit beginning the next month. Hugh threw out suggested places she could visit, and she pulled a small notebook from her purse to jot them down.

"I'll come in and wave you two off," she said when they reached the airport.

The first person Jake saw when he climbed out of the

limo was Clarissa. Two suitcases sat at her feet. She smiled nervously.

"Going somewhere?" he asked, conscious of Hugh and Marie joining him on the sidewalk, but focused on Clarissa.

"To Los Angeles. If the offer is still open."

"What offer?" Marie asked.

Hugh mumbled something, took her arm and led her inside the terminal.

Jake stepped closer.

"The offer will always be open." He kissed her softly, a quick brush against her lips. "What changed your mind?"

"When we talked last night in the garden."

"You can't fight fate?"

"I guess that has something to do with it. But mostly I was thinking how I admired you for taking a stand. Then last night I began to think how I should take a stand, take what I wanted—for however long it lasts."

"I am hoping it will last forever," he said softly, brushing his fingertips across her cheeks, gazing deep into her eyes.

Her heart skipped a beat. "Oh, Jake, I love you so much!" The words seem to burst from her heart.

Oh, no! She hadn't meant to say that! She had planned to accompany him to Los Angeles, have a torrid affair and leave when it was over without him ever knowing how she felt.

But instead of looking horrified at her exclamation, he kissed her. "I love you, too, Clarissa. I've wanted you in the worst way since that first day. Will you marry me?''

''Marriage? You and me? Oh, Jake, yes!''

''Even if it means living in Los Angeles with no trappings of royalty, no bowing footmen and grand receptions?''

She threw her arms around him, ignoring the gasp of the chauffeur. She didn't care who saw them, she loved this man and he loved her!

''I only want you! We'll have a wonderful life. I can still work for the women of Ambere from America. And with your contacts, I bet we can have them in full production in no time. I would want to come visit my family from time to time, but otherwise, where you go is where I want to be.''

He hugged her closely for a long moment. Then, growing conscious of the stares of everyone in sight, he slowly released her.

''We're gathering an audience.''

''Well, for the next few minutes, you are still Prince Jean-Antoine. Once we leave, you'll go back to plain Jake White. I bet no one would care if we kissed on the streets of L.A.''

''Only if we were blocking it.'' He laced his fingers through hers, and brought her hand up for a quick brush of lips over her fingers.

''I always wondered how a prince would know if a woman loved him for himself alone and not the trappings of royalty.''

''I don't,'' she began.

''I never thought you did.'' He squeezed her hand

gently. "And your coming here this morning proves it. However, the thing is, I've had a change in plans, as well."

"You don't want me to come to L.A?" She was stricken. Hadn't he just asked her to marry him?

"Oh, I want you in Los Angeles or anywhere else I am. We can get married right away, if you want. But maybe you'd rather come home to marry—have your father give you away. Have your mother cry at your wedding, and have your sisters be part of the wedding party."

Clarissa licked her lips and nodded. It was the kind of wedding she'd thought she'd have.

"I thought you weren't planning to return to Marique once we left today."

"That's the change of plan. I learned a lot last night, about family, my father, and some of the circumstances behind my grandfather's edicts. You were right. I can't fight fate. I do belong here. I like what I've seen of the country. I like the people I've met. I see a lot of potential for growth, for enjoying life in this country."

He looked into her eyes and smiled. Her heart kicked into high gear and she wanted to lean forward to kiss him, never mind the other passengers milling around.

"I'm going home to see what I can do to wind up my affairs in Los Angeles, but I'm coming back. If my grandfather and I can work things out, I guess there will be a ceremony making me crowned prince, after all. But not before I have a wife to become crowned princess."

"You're going to return? To take your place as prince?" Clarissa had never expected this!

"Is that a problem? Haven't you been after me to do that all along?"

"Yes, but that was before I said I'd marry you."

"And that would change anything how?"

"I can't marry a prince. I was engaged to one before. What would people think?"

"That you got a fairy-tale happy ending, after all."

"Or what you said back in L.A., that I was after the title and nothing else."

Jake roared with laughter. "Anyone who knows you would never think such a thing. And what do you care about the opinions of other people? Stand up for what you believe. Marry me, have children with me. Teach me how to get along with my grandfather. Help me rule our country together."

Clarissa stared at him. He was serious. Slowly the love blossomed until she was engulfed.

"Your wish is my command," she said, and despite years of training, of protocol and deportment, she leaned up to kiss her future husband right in front of a dozen strangers.

EPILOGUE

FIFTY years in the future a revered king would write a letter to his beloved wife on the occasion of their golden wedding anniversary fulfilling a long-held promise to let her know how his children—how their five children—turned out.

Nary a hell-raiser in the bunch!

Harlequin Romance®

is thrilled to present a lively new trilogy from

Jessica Hart:

City Brides

*They're on the career ladder,
but just one step away from the altar!*

Meet Phoebe, Kate and Bella…

These friends suddenly realize that they're fast approaching thirty and haven't yet found Mr. Right—or even Mr. Maybe!

But that's about to change. If fate won't lend a hand, they'll make their own luck. Whether it's a hired date or an engagement of convenience, they're determined that the next wedding invitation they see will be one of their own!

July—
FIANCÉ WANTED FAST!
(#3757)

August—
THE BLIND-DATE PROPOSAL
(#3761)

September—
THE WHIRLWIND ENGAGEMENT
(#3765)

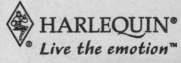

HARLEQUIN®
® *Live the emotion*™

Visit us at www.eHarlequin.com

HRCBJH3T

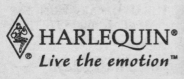

BETTY NEELS

Harlequin Romance® is proud to present this delightful story by Betty Neels. This wonderful novel is the climax of a unique career that saw Betty Neels become an international bestselling author, loved by millions of readers around the world.

A GOOD WIFE
(#3758)

Ivo van Doelen knew what he wanted—he simply needed to allow Serena Lightfoot time to come to the same conclusion. Now all he had to do was persuade Serena to accept his convenient proposal of marriage without her realizing he was already in love with her!

Don't miss this wonderful novel— brought to you by Harlequin Romance®!

HARLEQUIN®
Live the emotion™

Visit us at www.eHarlequin.com

HRBNAGWS